101
Questions & Answers
about the
UNIVERSE

101
Questions & Answers
about the
UNIVERSE

ROY A. GALLANT

MACMILLAN PUBLISHING COMPANY
NEW YORK
COLLIER MACMILLAN PUBLISHERS
LONDON

Macmillan Publishing Company
866 Third Avenue, New York, N.Y. 10022
Collier Macmillan Canada, Inc.
Diagrams by Science Photo/Graphics, Inc.
Printed in the United States of America
10   9   8   7   6   5   4   3   2   1
Library of Congress Cataloging in Publication Data
Gallant, Roy A.
101 questions and answers about the universe.
Includes index.
Summary: An introduction to astronomy using questions
actually asked by children at the Southworth Planetarium
in Maine.
1. Astronomy—Miscellanea—Juvenile literature.
[1. Astronomy. 2. Questions and answers] I. Title.
II. Title: One hundred one questions and answers about
the universe. III. Title: One hundred and one questions
and answers about the universe.
QB46.G28   1984   520   84-7875
ISBN 0-02-736750-9

For Jeannine

Contents

Next Question

This book was inspired by the thousands of young people who have attended the Southworth Planetarium at the University of Southern Maine over the past four years since I have had the privilege of being its director.

At the end of each planetarium show we have a question period during which the audience is invited to ask questions about the presentation, about the planetarium itself, or about astronomy in general. Nearly always the questions go on and on, which we like. While many can be anticipated and are of a routine nature ("How far away is Jupiter?" or "How many moons does Saturn have?" or "Which way to the rest rooms?"), many others show imagination and reflect a genuine interest in science ("Since there is lightning in Jupiter's upper clouds, and since the clouds are made of hydrogen, why doesn't Jupiter explode?"). Still others are simply funny ("I had a question but forgot it" or "How come you can show the stars in here when it's cloudy outside?" or "Does this place ever blow up?"). We can always count on some of the standard questions ("How much did the star machine cost, and how long did it take to build it?"). Another question often asked: "Does the ceiling open up?" I answer that it doesn't, adding that if it did there would be a lot of students falling down through the hole since there are classrooms overhead.

Each of the 101 questions answered in this book has been asked one or more times by elementary school groups regularly attending the planetarium. It is for those young people, and their teachers, that this book is written. Thank you one and all, especially those of you who submitted written questions and signed them.

Thank you . . . Jason Adilguard, Jenny Anthony, Trevor Atwell, David Bailey, Brooke Bishop, Sarah Buck, Breakwater School (Portland, Maine), C. K. Burns School (Saco, Maine), Philip Candelmo, Barbara Cleveland, Greg Cole, Chad Coleman, Gabriel Coognan, Consolidated School (Kennebunkport, Maine), Tina Cote, Cousins School (Kennebunk, Maine), Jennifer Curtis, Anthony Cushman, Shawn Darling, Richard Downs, Furham Elementary School (Lisbon, Maine), Matt Durloo, Carl Elliott, Emerson School (Sanford, Maine), Andy Estabrook, Erin Estey, Fairfield School (Saco, Maine), Field-Allen School (South Windham, Maine), Charles Fournier, Jennifer Fox, Sean Gallivan, Nicole Gaudreau, R. G., A. D. Gray Junior High School, Thomas Greer, Adam Hanlon, R. H., Holy Cross School (South Portland, Maine), Lisa Huggard, Jennifer Jackson, Kristen Jankowiak, Eric Johnson, Jordan Small Elementary School (Raymond, Maine), Clarice Kashinsky, Kings Junior High School (Portland, Maine), Larry, Jerry Livingston, Lyseth School (Portland, Maine), Lynda Maxwell, Randi McMann, Memorial Junior High School (South Portland, Maine), Memorial School (North Yarmouth, Maine), Brenda Mumma, Amy O'Connor, Park Street School (Kennebunk, Maine), Carl Peterson, Darren Peterson, Amy R., Reiche School (Portland, Maine), the Recks family, Benjamin Richardson, Jessica Roberge, Room 5, Rowe School (Yarmouth, Maine), Russel School (Gray, Maine), Sanford Middle School (Sanford, Maine), Brandi-Jo Sangillo, Tara Spade, Aaron Sypek, Daniel Tarkinson, Christopher Thurston, Adam Walbridge, Michael Westort, Nate Wilmot, David White, Yarmouth Intermediate School (Yarmouth, Maine), York Elementary School (York, Maine), and Gregg Zimmerman.

I wish also to thank Dr. K. L. Franklin, astronomer, friend, colleague, and former Chairman of The American Museum–Hayden Planetarium, New York City, for his helpful suggestions on his review of the manuscript of this book. My thanks also to Jeannine L. Dickey for her assistance on the computer in the manuscript preparation of the book. And finally, my thanks to Dr. Robert J. Hatala, Dean of the College of Arts and Sciences, the University of Southern Maine, for his encouragement to proceed with this project.

1 What is a comet? and Why does the tail of a comet always face away from the Sun?

Comets are dirty snowballs from space, or so they have been called by some astronomers. There are billions of them in the deep cold of space about 140 trillion miles out from the Sun. That's far beyond Pluto, the most distant planet (see Question 34). The comets seem to occupy an immense spherical volume of space enclosing the Sun and all the planets. Like the planets, comets are held as captives of the Sun by the Sun's gravitation, so they are part of the Solar System. Comets are a mixture of rock dust and ice. At the center is the *nucleus,* a loose lump of rock dust and ice that may be from about 1 to 50 or so miles across. Once in a while, a passing star's gravitational attraction flings a comet toward the Sun. When the comet nears the Sun, the nucleus is heated and some of the ice turns to gas. A ball of gas forms around the nucleus and swells up to many times larger than Earth. It is called the *coma.* Some comets develop tails thousands or millions of miles long. One part of the tail usually is a yellowish color and is made of rock dust freed when some of the ice turned to gas. A second part of the tail may be bluish and is made of atoms of the gas carbon monoxide. A wind of trillions of bits and pieces of atoms blowing out from the Sun keeps a comet's tail always pointed away from the Sun (see Question 76).

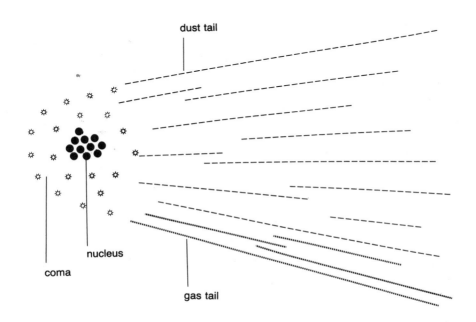

dust tail

nucleus

coma

gas tail

2 Where do the stars go during the day?

They don't go anywhere. The stars are in the sky during the day as well as during the night. We say that the stars "come out" at night. We begin to see the brightest stars at sunset when the sky begins to darken. The darker the sky gets, the more stars we can see. Then at sunrise the sky once again grows light, and the stars fade from view. We lose sight of the dimmer stars first, then the brighter ones. On a very clear day you can sometimes see the Moon at mid-morning or mid-afternoon. Sometimes you can even see the planet Venus in the daytime if you know just where to look. But the stars appear too faint to be seen in the bright sky of day.

3 What makes the stars twinkle?

The air is moving all the time. Since the air holds a lot of dust and smoke particles, which we sometimes see as smog, the particles are kept dancing about by the moving air. As light from the stars shines down through the air with its dancing dust and smoke particles, the light dims a little and then brightens again. This happens very quickly and so makes the stars seem to twinkle. It is like looking at a distant streetlight at night with a thick cloud of moths flying around the light bulb. Another reason for the stars twinkling is that air moved past us by the wind is not all the same density. Because small parcels of air vary in density, neighboring parcels passing between us and a star we may be looking at refract, or bend, the star's light by different amounts. Called *scintillation*, this action of the air also causes the stars to twinkle.

At one time, comets (like this one with a tail several million miles long) were regarded as signs of evil. Centuries ago, the Romans thought of comets as souls on their way to heaven. (Lick Observatory)

4 What are meteorites made of, and what makes a meteor?

Between the orbits of Mars and Jupiter are millions of chunks of rock and metal called the *asteroids*. Astronomers once thought that the asteroids might be the remains of a planet that was shattered by Jupiter's powerful gravitation, but the asteroids probably are material left over from the time the planets were formed.

When asteroids smash into each other from time to time they shatter into many smaller pieces. These smaller pieces fly off into new orbits that take them on paths that cross the orbits of the planets. We call these bits and pieces of smashed asteroids *meteoroids*.

Meteoroids enter Earth's air at speeds from 10 to 45 miles a second. Because they fall so fast they get very hot and flare up as brief streaks of light we call *meteors*. If a meteoroid survives its blazing journey down through the air and hits the ground, it is called a *meteorite*. Some are made of rock (silicate) and are called *stony* meteorites. Others are made of metal (iron and nickel) and are called *iron* meteorites. And still others are part rock and part metal and are called *stony-iron* meteorites.

Before astronomers discovered where meteorites come from, people thought they were stars falling out of the sky. You still hear the terms "falling stars" and "shooting stars." On a clear night out in the country away from the glare of city lights, you can see about five meteors an hour. About 10 tons of high-speed meteor dust rain down through Earth's air every day. About 400 tons of tiny meteorites, called *micrometeorites,* fall to the ground each day.

5 What are some of the largest meteorites ever found?

The largest known meteorite, called the Hoba West, fell on Botswana, in

above: *The Wilamette meteorite, on display at The American Museum—Hayden Planetarium in New York City, is the remains of a meteoroid that was sculptured by frictional heating when it blazed through Earth's atmosphere as a meteor. It is solid metal and weighs 14.5 tons.* (Courtesy The American Museum—Hayden Planetarium)

left: *This is a drawing of the Leonid meteor shower of November 13, 1833. One observer said at the time, "The stars fell like flakes of snow." Another, also believing that meteors were stars, thought that there would be no stars left in the sky the next night.* (Courtesy The American Museum—Hayden Planetarium)

southwestern Africa, and weighs about 60 tons, the weight of about 20 pickup trucks. The second largest is the Ahnighito meteorite, weighing about half that much (34 tons). It was found in Cape York, Greenland, and was shipped to New York City by Admiral Peary. It is on display at The American Museum of Natural History in New York City.

About 20,000 years ago a much larger meteorite crashed into the Arizona desert. It was about the size of a railroad car and blasted out a hole almost a mile across and nearly 600 feet deep. The meteorite exploded into many pieces when it struck. There are about 80 known large meteorite craters on Earth. But there must be many more.

⑥ What is a meteor shower, and what causes one?

Several times a year we are treated to grand displays of meteors raining down on us in showers. These *shower* meteors occur pretty much on schedule. A particular shower is named after the constellation it appears to be coming from. For example, the Orionids appear to fan out of the constellation Orion the hunter in late October at the rate of about 25 meteors an hour. Shower meteors seem to be the remains of old comets that have been broken down into small pieces by the heat of the Sun. There are about 10 major meteor showers and 14 minor showers each year.

A SELECTION OF MAJOR METEOR SHOWERS

Name of Shower	Best Viewing Time	Number of Meteors Per Hour	How Long They Last (in days)
Quadrantids	January 4	40	1
Aquarids	May 4	20	3
Aquarids	July 28	20	7
Perseids	August 11	50	5
Orionids	October 21	25	2
Geminids	December 13	50	3

7 How many stars are there?

On a clear night, from either the Northern or Southern Hemisphere you can see about 4,500 stars with the unaided eye—for a total of about 9,000 stars. Binoculars bring a few thousand more into view. A three-inch telescope reveals about half a million. But there are many more stars than that. The Milky Way galaxy, which is our home galaxy and probably an average-size one (see Question 13), may have more than 500 billion stars. Since our galaxy is only one of billions of other galaxies, there must be trillions upon trillions of stars, more than anyone could count in a lifetime.

8 What makes the stars move across the sky?

The stars only seem to parade across the sky each night, rising in the east and setting in the west. They do not actually move that way. That "motion" is caused by Earth's turning on its axis like a very slowly spinning top. Because we are carried along by Earth's spinning surface, the stars, Sun, and Moon all appear to move across the sky. Astronomers call that motion *apparent motion*. Until the 1550s most people believed that Earth stood still and that the apparent motion of the stars was their real motion. The stars actually do move in relation to each other, but they are so very far away we cannot see their real motions of many miles a second.

9 What is a constellation, and can people really see pictures in the constellations?

Stargazers of very long ago invented the constellations, which include Orion the hunter, Leo the lion, Taurus the bull, and many others. Don't be dis-

Just before dark, the lights of a village appear as shown in this sketch. The more distant a street light, the fainter it appears to the eye (left). At right is how our village-constellation appears when darkness falls. This is how the various stars forming a given constellation actually are arranged in space—some nearer, others farther away. (Courtesy Larousse Astronomy)

appointed if you can't make out the fanciful figures as they are shown in books. No one else can, either. Today, astronomers list a total of 88 constellations. This sky zoo of star groups includes 19 land animals, 13 humans, 10 water creatures, nine birds, a couple of centaurs, a dragon, a unicorn, and a head of hair. The stars in a constellation are not arranged flat, like dots on a blackboard, but in three dimensions, like leaves on a tree. The constellations are beautifully false figures. Because the stars move in relation to one another, all the constellations are gradually changing their shapes. But this happens so slowly that we cannot see a constellation change in our lifetime. What good are the constellations? They serve as an excellent way for you to find your way around the night sky, and as illustrations for the old myths.

10 What is the Zodiac?

Stargazers of long ago observed that the Sun, Moon, and planets all seemed to move along an imaginary highway forming a complete circle around the

An old drawing of the constellation Orion the hunter. Notice the two stars marking his shoulders, the three marking his belt, the small group marking the middle of his sword, one marking his right ankle, and another marking his left knee. Orion holds a lion's hide shield in his right hand and a club in his left hand.

sky. This circular band was called the *Zodiac* and its center line was called the *ecliptic*. While the Sun traveled exactly along the ecliptic, the planets moved along within the band. The Zodiac band contains 12 evenly spaced constellations (see Question 9) in this order: Aries (the ram), Taurus (the bull), Gemini (the twins), Cancer (the crab), Leo (the lion), Virgo (the virgin), Libra (the scales), Scorpius (the scorpion), Sagittarius (the archer), Capricorn (the sea-goat), Aquarius (the water-carrier), and Pisces (the fishes).

11 Is there a difference between astronomy and astrology?

Astronomy is the science dealing with the stars, planets, and other celestial bodies, their distances, brightness, size, motions, what they are made of, and how they are put together. The word "astronomy" comes from the Greek and means "the arrangement of the stars." *Astrology* is an extremely old belief that the positions of the stars and planets in relation to each other, and their motions, have a controlling influence over the kind of person you are, what kind of work you do, your health, moods, wealth, and so on. It also is supposed to have a controlling influence over animals, plants, nations, and institutions such as IBM and the League of Women Voters. Astrology is a superstition, not a science.

12 What is a light-year?

A *light-year* is a measure of distance and is based on the speed of light. It is the distance light travels in one year, at the rate of 186,282 miles a second. That amounts to about 6 trillion miles. Distances across space between stars and galaxies are so great that units of measure such as the mile are too small to work with conveniently. For example, it is easier to say that our closest neighboring star, in the Alpha Centauri system, is 4.3 light-years away than to write 25,278,000,000,000 miles.

13 What's a galaxy?

A *galaxy* is a vast collection of stars, planets, gas, and dust held together by gravitation (see Question 41). There are *spiral* galaxies, like the Andromeda Galaxy and like the one we live in, which have spiral arms like a Fourth of July pinwheel. These galaxies are very bright and have a central region (the nucleus) packed with many stars. There also are *barred spiral* galaxies, which have arms reaching outward from the ends of a central bar. *Elliptical*

above: *This galaxy, photographed through the 200-inch telescope, is seen in the constellation Virgo. Notice its spherical central region of stars, called the nucleus, surrounded by a dense rim of stars containing dark bands of gas and dust.* (Hale Observatories)

left: *The Andromeda Galaxy with its two companion satellite galaxies, as photographed through the 200-inch telescope. It is regarded as a near twin of our home galaxy, the Milky Way, because both are spiral galaxies.* (Hale Observatories)

galaxies are slightly flattened, sphere-shaped galaxies. *Irregular* galaxies have no regular shape. Two neighbor galaxies of ours, called the Clouds of Magellan, are both irregular galaxies. Galaxies are huge cities of stars that measure hundreds and thousands of light-years across (see Question 12). They contain hundreds of billions of stars and probably even greater numbers of planets.

14 Is there just one galaxy?

No. The Universe contains billions upon billions of galaxies (see Question 13). The galaxies are spread out everywhere in space and seem to go on forever. If you had a powerful telescope and looked just in the bowl region of the Big Dipper, you would see more than half a million galaxies, and the bowl region of the Big Dipper is only a tiny patch of the entire sky.

15 What is the Milky Way?

From ancient times stargazers have noticed a hazy band of light stretching across the sky from horizon to horizon. Many regarded it as the "path to heaven." The Greeks named it the *Milky Way,* and in their myths thought of it as milk spilled by the goddess Hera as she nursed the infant Heracles, or Hercules.

As early as the fifth century B.C., the Greek philosopher Democritus thought that it was a band of many stars. In the early 1600s, the Italian astronomer Galileo, who was the first to study the stars with a telescope, showed that Democritus was right. By studying the shape of the Milky Way, other astronomers correctly thought that the Sun and its planets were part of a vast

This picture is made up of several photographs put together to form a single photograph of the Milky Way as we see it in the summer sky. The view extends from the constellation Sagittarius to Cassiopeia. The dark band, or rift, is a dark cloud of gas and dust that prevents us from seeing the bright central region of the galaxy. (Hale Observatories)

Hundreds of craters, some with bright white rays such as the two at center, can be seen in this photograph of the Moon taken at last quarter. The large sprawling dark areas are maria, "oceans" of dark rock that long ago flowed up out of the Moon as molten lava and froze. (Lick Observatory)

collection of stars in the shape of a huge powder puff. That grouping of stars came to be called a galaxy (see Question 13) with the name of the Milky Way.

16 Why do meteors make holes in the Moon?

In the early history of the Solar System there must have been countless thousands of asteroid-size (see Question 4) lumps of rock and metal being swept up gravitationally by the newly formed planets. As these rock bombs smashed into the Moon (and other planets) over the centuries, they struck with such force that they blasted out large chunks of the Moon's surface rock and formed craters. Some of the Moon's craters have walls four miles high, with central peaks, and measure many miles across. The giant crater Copernicus is 55 miles across. The Moon's craters come in many sizes. Some are smaller than a dime and were made by tiny high-speed meteoroids.

17 How did the Moon get its mountains?

Astronomers think that the Moon's mountains were formed soon after the Moon was formed. At that time, more than four billion years ago, its surface rock was very hot and slowly cooled. As it cooled, it cracked apart in some places and crumpled up in others, forcing huge, heaving masses of rock thousands of feet into the air. But most of the Moon's mountains are the rims of large, dark areas of frozen lava called *maria*, or seas. The Moon's mountains still have the sharp edges and peaks they had when they were formed. The reason is that there is no water or wind on the Moon to wear them smooth, as our Earth mountains have been worn smooth by centuries of erosion. The Moon has chains of mountains that run for hundreds of miles. One, called the Apennines, is 400 miles long and is located in the north-central section of the Moon's disk. The Moon's highest visible peak, Mount Leibnitz, is about 35,000 feet high. It is near the Moon's south pole.

18 What are the big dark patches I can see when I look at the Moon through binoculars?

They are called *maria* (see Question 17). But they are seas of black volcanic rock, not seas of water. Because these vast patches of rock are dark, they reflect less of the Sun's light than do the surrounding regions of lighter rock, and so the maria appear dark. Maria cover about half of the Moon's surface and have been given very colorful names, such as the Sea of Showers (700 miles wide and the largest sea), the Ocean of Storms, the Sea of Clouds, and the Sea of Crises. The maria probably were formed early in the Moon's life when it had a thin crust of rock, beneath which was molten rock. While the Moon's craters were being formed (see Question 16) by large chunks of rock striking the crust with explosive force, one or more especially large pieces may have smashed right through the Moon's thin crust. This would have opened large pockets in the crustal rock and let the molten rock, lava, beneath spill out and flow over large areas of the surface. Eventually these lava spills cooled and became the black rock we see today.

19 What makes the Moon's shape change?

Once a month, or about every 28 days, the Moon travels in a complete circle around Earth. As it does, it goes through *phases* and appears to change shape. This is because we on Earth see only that part of the Moon that catches the Sun's light. Look at the diagram as you read on. When the Sun, Moon, and Earth are in a straight line, with the Moon in the middle, we don't see the Moon at all since the side facing us is in shadow (position M_1 in the diagram). At this point the Moon is said to be "new." As the Moon circles Earth we begin to see part of its surface reflecting sunlight. First we see it as a crescent and then as a half moon (position M_2). As the Moon keeps moving around and reaches the point opposite its new-moon position (position M_3) we see a full moon. We see another half moon when the Moon swings around to position M_4.

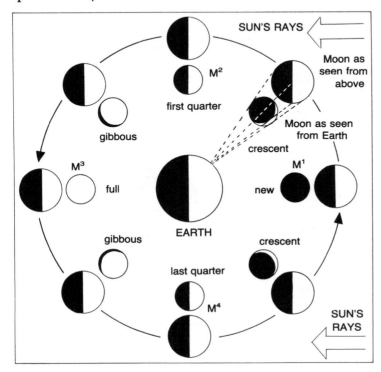

From Earth we see the Moon go through "phases," represented by the inner rim of moons in the diagram. But if you were in space above Earth's North Pole, the Moon would always appear to be half full (you would see only the outer rim), as would Earth. (Courtesy Cathie Polgreen)

20 Is it true that a full moon makes you go crazy?

No. If that were true we'd all be crazy, since there is a full moon once every month (see Question 19). Many years ago there was a superstition that the phases of the Moon affected the lives of people, especially the full moon. People spoke of "Moon madness," or "lunacy." The words "lunacy" and "lunatic" come from the Latin word for Moon, *luna*. So-called Moon madness came from observations that mental patients were especially restless during the full moon. This was so not because of any supernatural force of the Moon, but because of the Moon's greater light during its full phase. This made sleep more difficult and caused the patients to be more active than usual.

21 Is the flag astronaut Neil Armstrong put up on the Moon still there?

Most likely it is, since the other American astronauts didn't take it down,

and since no other nation has been to the Moon. Another reason that it probably is where Armstrong planted it is that there is no wind on the Moon to blow it down, since the Moon does not have air. Without an atmosphere there cannot be rain to gully the surface. About the only natural force that could knock the flag down would be a violent moonquake. We won't know for sure that the flag is still standing until other astronauts visit that part of the Moon first explored by Neil Armstrong and Edwin Aldrin, Jr., on July 20, 1969.

22 How did Earth get the Moon?

Astronomers are not sure, but they have some ideas. The Moon probably was formed right along with Earth out of masses of gas and dust that were part of the super-cloud of matter out of which the Sun formed (see Questions 23, 25, and 77). Gravitation within the Moon-cloud matter would have packed the matter tighter and tighter around the core region. The cloud matter then condensed, or turned into solid rock. The rock then heated up, melted, and eventually cooled to become the Moon we see today.

It was once thought that the Moon was torn out of Earth's crust and deeper rock layer when Earth was young, and that the Pacific Ocean basin is the old scar. Another theory, also no longer favored, is that the Moon is a captured world that once orbited the Sun on its own. It seems very unlikely that Earth could have captured the Moon and held onto it. Instead, the Moon would have been briefly attracted but then gravitationally flung away from Earth. Furthermore, if the Moon were a captured planet, its orbit would be a long, stretched-out one—like that of Pluto (see Questions 43 and 65)—instead of the nearly circular one it is today.

Neil Armstrong after planting the American flag on the Moon's surface in 1969. (NASA)

23 How was Earth made?

Earth had a stormy and fiery beginning. Astronomers tell us that about 4.6 billion years ago there was a huge cloud of gas and dust spinning around in the form of a disk, stretching out from the infant Sun (see Question 25). Tiny dust grains of the disk material collided and began clumping together. Clumps attracted other clumps until the disk contained many billions of solid objects, ranging from a few inches to many feet in size. Some of the solid clumps were made of ices, others of rocky material, and still others contained metals including iron, for example. Called *planetesimals,* these clumps of disk material collected into giant globes that became Earth and the other planets and their moons. The primitive Earth-ball grew larger and more massive as it attracted and swept up more planetesimals in a process called *accretion.*

The matter in the core region of infant Earth was under such great pressure that temperatures there rose very high. Heat was also being released by radioactivity. At that time Earth must have been a soupy globe of rock and metal about 2,000° C. Free to flow about, these rock and metal materials separated. The heavier iron and nickel sank into the core region. The lighter rock matter, *silicates*, floated to the surface. So Earth developed a crust of lightweight rocky matter, which surrounds a core of superdense iron and nickel.

As the rock crust cooled, large planetesimals continued to smash into Earth, scarring its surface with deep craters like those visible today on Mercury, Mars, and the Moon. Because the crust was no longer molten when these late-arrival planetesimals, containing large amounts of heavy metals, struck the surface, the metals remained part of Earth's crust instead of sinking into the core region. Although no one can say for certain that Earth and the other planets were formed just that way, all the evidence we have points to some such process.

24 How did Earth get its air?

When Earth was a soupy mass of hot rock and metal (see Question 23), many gases bubbled out and collected above the new planet as a primitive atmosphere. Among them there probably were large amounts of hydrogen, water vapor, nitrogen, carbon monoxide, and carbon dioxide, as well as smaller amounts of methane, ammonia, and hydrogen sulfide. Energy from the Sun broke down some of these gases. It changed ammonia into free hydrogen and nitrogen. Methane was changed into carbon and hydrogen, and water vapor was changed into hydrogen and oxygen. The free hydrogen was so light that most of it escaped Earth's gravitational grip. Many such chemical changes must have taken place in that atmosphere. So, if scientists are correct, some 400 million years after our planet had developed a solid, cool crust, it had an atmosphere mostly of carbon dioxide, carbon monoxide, water vapor, methane, and ammonia. Oxygen, which today makes up 21 percent of the air, did not collect in large amounts until green plants evolved. Green plants keep our air supplied with oxygen.

25 How was the Sun made?

Astronomers tell us that some 4.6 billion years ago the Sun and its planets formed out of a huge cloud of gas and dust about 20 billion miles across. Gravitational attraction of matter at the center of the cloud drew the cloud inward. This packing of matter in the core region of the cloud caused it to heat up. As the cloud contracted it began to spin and cast off a huge rotating disk. About 90 percent of the cloud's gas and dust formed a sphere at the center of the disk. The densely packed globe of matter eventually began to glow a dull red due to heating. The heating resulted from the high pressure caused by a steady rain of matter down into the Sun's core region. Eventually,

19

when the temperature rose to about 10 million degrees, the Sun began to shine with the yellowish white light we see today. Although no one can say for certain that the Sun (and all other stars) formed just that way, evidence points to some such process.

26 What makes the Sun shine?

(Before reading the answer to this question, read the answer to Question 25.) The Sun produces an enormous amount of energy. In one second the Sun pours out more energy than people have used since there have been people on this planet. Yet Earth receives only about one billionth of the Sun's energy output. How can any object produce so much energy? And to do so, what must that object be made of?

The Sun releases energy in the form of X rays, ultraviolet rays, visible light, infrared radiation, and radio waves. All of this energy is produced deep within the Sun's core region. The core gases are under tremendous pressure because they are squeezed by the overlying weight of other gases closer to the surface. The core is squeezed so tightly that it is about 10 times denser than silver. High pressure in the core region means high temperature as well— about 15 million degrees. When the temperature is that high, atoms cannot remain whole. They break apart into their individual pieces—*protons, neutrons,* and *electrons.* So deep within the Sun there are no whole atoms, only a superdense sea of mostly protons and electrons.

The Sun is made mostly of the gas hydrogen, each atom of which has one proton and one electron. A hydrogen atom's single proton forms the nucleus of the atom. So there are lots of free protons, or hydrogen nuclei, tightly packed in the Sun's core. When two protons bump into each other with enough force, they fuse into a single lump of matter. As they do, part of their mass is changed into energy. The single lump next fuses with another free proton, and another tiny burst of energy is given off. A series of such fusions eventually builds the nucleus of a helium atom, which is a clump of two protons and two neutrons.

At each step along the way, energy is produced in the form of *photons*. In brief, the Sun shines by fusing hydrogen atom nuclei into the nuclei of helium atoms. The photons of energy produced during fusion in the Sun's core take 50 million years to work their way up to the Sun's surface, a distance of some 432,000 miles. It then takes that energy only eight minutes to cross space and reach Earth, a distance of 93 million miles.

27 How long can the Sun keep shining?

Like any other star, the Sun cannot keep shining forever. As far as we can tell, it has been shining for about 4.6 billion years and it is about halfway through its life span. That means that it should keep shining for about another 4.6 billion years, if it keeps shining as it does today. The Sun shines by fusing hydrogen into helium (see Question 26). Since there is only a limited

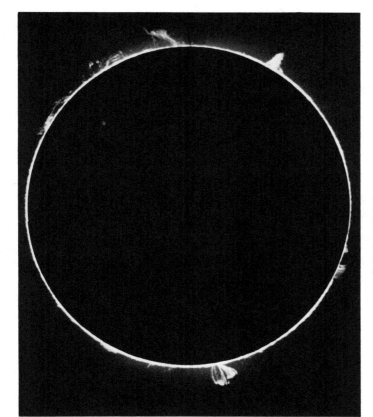

Like other stars, the "fiery" Sun is extremely active. In this photograph most of the Sun's disk has been blocked out to reveal several eruptive surface features called prominences. (Hale Observatories)

amount of hydrogen in the Sun's core region to serve as fuel for shining, the Sun must stop shining as we see it today when it uses up its core hydrogen fuel supply.

The Sun is able to keep shining throughout a very long life span of about 10 billion years because it takes very little mass (hydrogen nuclei) to produce an enormous amount of energy. For example, if a rock or a piece of wood with a mass of only about two pounds were turned completely into energy, it would supply all the electricity needs of the United States for about two months.

28 What kinds of gases are in the Sun?

By studying the Sun's light through a prismlike instrument called a *spectroscope,* astronomers have learned what the Sun is made of. It is a ball of gas containing many of the chemical elements known to us on Earth. But most of the Sun is hydrogen gas (about 78 percent) with about 20 percent helium, and about 2 percent oxygen, carbon, nitrogen, neon, nickel, silicon, sulfur, iron, and other elements in smaller amounts.

29 What happens when the Sun's gases go out?

All stars, including the Sun, one day must stop shining when they have used up their hydrogen fuel (see Question 27). In about 4.6 billion years the Sun will have exhausted its core hydrogen fuel supply. When that happens, the core gradually sends less and less energy up toward the surface so the core begins to cool. A cooling core is a core with decreasing pressure. The star then collapses in on itself. This sudden gravitational infall of matter into the core temporarily sends the temperature and pressure zooming. The Sun will then swell up and shine as a huge star, with a reddish light, called a *red giant* star.

The core temperature will become high enough so that the helium there is fused into carbon and other elements. The burst of heat caused by the collapse also causes a shell of hydrogen just outside the core to fuse into helium, so the red giant's furnace is still blazing away. But because the Sun will then lack enough mass to keep the temperature high, the fusions will stop and the Sun will again collapse, this time into a small star called a *white dwarf*, not much larger than Earth. The white dwarf Sun will shine with an intense white light for a while. But gradually it will dim and darken, ending its long life as a cold dark body called a *black dwarf*.

30 Why is the Sun yellow?

By examining the color of the Sun's surface, astronomers can make a pretty good guess about its temperature, which is about 6,000 (Kelvin) degrees. (Kelvin degrees are used on the absolute temperature scale. On that scale 0° K is equal to −273.1° C or −460° F.) You know from experience that as a charcoal fire is allowed to go out, its coals change from white hot to orange hot to red hot as they cool off. And an object that glows bluish white is hotter than a white-hot object.

As we look about us in the night sky and see stars of different colors, we know that the blue white ones, such as Rigel in the constellation Orion, are among the hottest ones. They have surface temperatures around 50,000 (Kelvin) degrees. The yellowish white ones like the Sun are medium hot, 6,000 (Kelvin) degrees. The reddish stars, such as Betelgeuse in the constellation Orion, have much cooler surfaces of about 3,000 (Kelvin) degrees. So a star with a surface temperature around 6,000 degrees shines with a yellowish white light. All the yellowish white stars we see in the sky, such as Capella in the constellation Auriga, are Sun-like stars.

31 Why is the Sun a star?

A *star* is a hot, glowing globe of gas that emits light and other energy by a process of fusion in its core region (see Question 27). The Sun is a typical, and the closest, star. Most stars are enormous compared with planets, containing enough matter to make thousands of Earth-like planets.

A *planet* is a celestial object that shines by reflected light from a star to which it is held gravitationally captive and about which it revolves. There are nine known primary planets in the Solar System. Whether a celestial object is to be a star or planet depends entirely on how much mass, or matter, the object has when it is formed.

Jupiter is especially interesting in this respect. Jupiter is two and a half times more massive than all of the other planets combined. It also emits more energy than it receives from the Sun. We can imagine a time in the Solar System's youth when the giant planet might have rivaled the Sun as a possible star. Like the Sun, Jupiter was a huge cloud of gas that contracted and began heating up. But Jupiter lacked enough mass to send its core temperature high enough to start the fusion of hydrogen into helium. The core probably heated up to only a few tens of thousands of degrees, a far cry from the 10 million degrees needed for fusion reactions. Even so, Jupiter probably grew hot enough so that it glowed red and resembled a red dwarf star. It radiated enough heat to warm and light its inner moons for many centuries. But the near-star was destined to fade as it cooled, and it continues to cool today.

32 Is the Sun the biggest star in the Universe?

No. Many stars are larger than the Sun. Such stars are red giants, blue giants, and supergiants. Betelgeuse, in the constellation Orion the hunter, is a giant star 400 times larger than the Sun. If Betelgeuse replaced the Sun as our local star, it would swallow up Mercury, Venus, and Earth, and would fill up the Solar System out to the orbit of Mars. And Betelgeuse is not an especially large star. A star called Epsilon Aurigae is 5,000 times larger than the Sun. If Epsilon Aurigae were our local star, it would fill up the Solar System to about halfway between Saturn and Uranus.

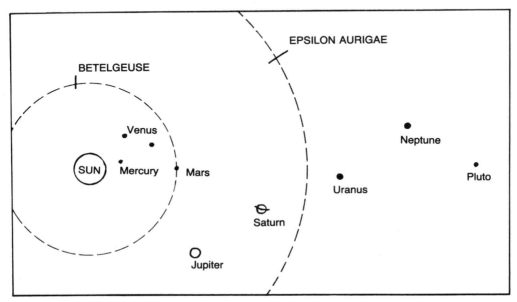

Many stars are larger than the Sun. Here the Sun is compared in size with the stars Betelgeuse and Epsilon Aurigae.

33 How hot is it in the Sun?

The surface gases of the Sun are about 6,000 degrees (Kelvin). Temperatures inside the Sun rise sharply in the gases deeper down. The temperature of the gases in the core region of the Sun is about 15 million degrees. The Sun is so hot that a spaceship could not examine it from a close-up view. The spaceship and everything in it would be vaporized, or turned into atoms.

There are many stars that are much hotter than the Sun. The blue giant stars have surface temperatures of 50,000 degrees and more, and core temperatures of many millions of degrees.

34 How far is the Sun from Earth?

The Sun's distance from Earth is 92,960,000 miles. To drive that distance at 60 miles an hour would take 177 years. A jet plane traveling along at 450 miles an hour would get you there a bit quicker—in 24 years. Here is the Sun's distance from the other planets:

AVERAGE DISTANCE OF THE PLANETS FROM THE SUN	
Planet	Distance (in miles)
Mercury	47,163,000
Venus	67,235,000
Earth	92,960,000
Mars	141,614,000
Asteroids	313,000,000
Jupiter	483,600,000
Saturn	886,700,000
Uranus	1,783,000,000
Neptune	2,794,000,000
Pluto	3,666,000,000

The Solar System is mostly empty space, as you can see in this diagram, which shows the relative distances of the planets from the Sun.

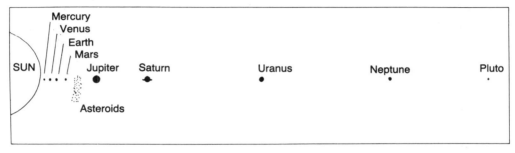

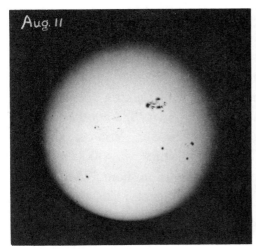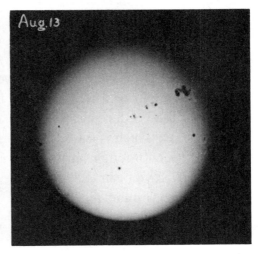

Sunspots—magnetic disturbances seen in the Sun's surface gases—last from a few hours to several days and occur in cycles. As the Sun rotates on its axis, sunspots are carried around, as shown in these two photographs of the Sun taken two days apart. (Yerkes Observatory)

35 What are sunspots?

Sunspots are huge areas of extremely powerful magnetic fields seen in the Sun's surface gases. A typical large sunspot is five times Earth's size. They appear dark because their gases are cooler than surrounding gases. Sunspots occur in regular cycles of about 11 years and are associated with an ''active'' Sun. Most of these upwellings of gases appear about a third of the way between the Sun's equator and poles and have a life of a few hours to several days. Sunspot activity causes changes in Earth's climate. Glaciers on Earth have come and gone in step with sunspot cycles over the past 7,000 years. An active Sun causes the glaciers to retreat. A quiet Sun causes them to advance.

36 How fast is Earth moving?

The next time you're out jogging and someone who passes you tells you that you are moving too slowly, you can say that actually you are moving quite fast enough. If you were jogging along at 5 miles an hour at the equator, your speed would be 1,038 miles an hour (plus your jogging speed), since that is how fast Earth rotates at the equator. Next you can add another 67,000 miles an hour, which is Earth's speed as it circles the Sun. You can also add the Sun's speed through our local group of stars, which is 44,000 miles an hour, and then you can tack on another 600,000 miles an hour, which is the group's speed around the galaxy. So you're moving at 712,043 miles an hour!

37 How fast does Saturn go as it orbits the Sun?

Here are the speeds of all of the planets as they orbit the Sun. What pattern do you notice in their speeds?

SPEEDS OF THE PLANETS AS THEY REVOLVE AROUND THE SUN

Planet	Speed (in miles per hour)
Mercury	107,376
Venus	78,295
Earth	67,109
Mars	53,687
Jupiter	29,080
Saturn	21,600
Uranus	15,212
Neptune	12,080
Pluto	10,515

38 Why is the Sun in the middle of the Universe?

The Sun isn't in the middle of the Universe. However, until about the year

1600 most people, including astronomers, thought that Earth was at the center of the Universe. Since they could not feel Earth move as it rotated on its axis and revolved about the Sun, people thought that Earth was motionless in space. Another reason for thinking this was that the Bible said that Earth does not move.

The reason for thinking that Earth was at the center of the Universe was the apparent daily motion of the Sun across the sky, and the apparent motion of the stars across the sky by night (see Question 8). Earth seemed to stand still while all other objects in the Universe moved around it. In the mid-1500s the Polish astronomer Nicolaus Copernicus published a book that explained that the Sun and stars actually do not move around Earth. Earth's rotation on its axis creates this false motion. He further explained that Earth and the other planets then known all revolve around the Sun, so Earth could not be the center of things. And as we know today, neither could the Sun be the center of the Universe—although it is the center of the Solar System—since it is located out near the edge of our galaxy, nowhere near the center.

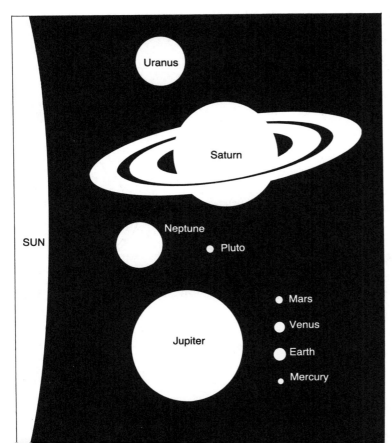

Compare Earth's size with that of the other planets and the Sun. How many of the other planets are larger than Earth?

39 How big are the Sun and planets?

The Sun is the largest, and most massive, object in the Solar System. Jupiter is the second largest and second most massive. It has more than twice the mass of all the other planets combined. While almost 10 Jupiters could be lined up across the face of the Sun, it would take 109 Earths to reach from one edge of the Sun to the other. Eleven Earths could be lined up across Jupiter's face. The diameters, or distances across, the Sun and planets are shown below. (Notice that we are not certain about Pluto's size, since it is so small and so very far away.)

SIZES OF THE SUN AND PLANETS

Object	Diameter (in miles)
Sun	865,000
Jupiter	88,983
Saturn	74,500
Uranus	32,190
Neptune	25,150
Earth	7,926
Venus	7,520
Mars	4,222
Mercury	3,032
Pluto	1,500(?)

40 What planets have the biggest moons?

Jupiter has the largest moon in the Solar System. It is Ganymede, which is larger than Mercury. Saturn's moon Titan is the second largest in the Solar System and is also larger than Mercury. So is Triton, which circles Neptune and is the third largest. The sizes of several other moons are shown here:

SIZES OF A SELECTION OF MAJOR MOONS

Moon	Planet	Diameter (in miles)
Ganymede	Jupiter	3,275
Titan	Saturn	3,195
Triton	Neptune	3,000
Callisto	Jupiter	2,995
Io	Jupiter	2,255
Moon	Earth	2,160
Europa	Jupiter	1,945
Oberon	Uranus	1,015
Titania	Uranus	995
Rhea	Saturn	950
Iapetus	Saturn	895
Dione	Saturn	895
Ariel	Uranus	825
Umbriel	Uranus	690
Tethys	Saturn	650
Ceres	an asteroid	620

Io is the most fascinating moon in the Solar System. It has several active volcanoes, which continually change Io's surface features. About the size of our Moon, Io as seen here was photographed by Voyager 1 from a distance of about half a million miles. (NASA)

41 What makes the planets go around the Sun? and Why don't the planets fall into the Sun?

Because of their speed, planets don't fall into the Sun. If you shoot a gun at the distant horizon, the bullet does not go over the horizon but falls to the ground. A projectile from a large cannon travels several miles before falling to the ground. Now imagine a supercannon that can give its projectile so much speed that the projectile falls right over the horizon. As the projectile moves forward it also falls toward the ground by a certain amount. But it never reaches the ground because Earth's surface curves away by exactly the same amount that the projectile falls.

This principle explains why artificial satellites and the Moon stay in orbit around Earth, and why the planets stay in orbit around the Sun. For every 670 miles the Moon moves forward in its orbit around Earth, it falls a distance of nine feet. But because Earth's surface also curves away by nine feet during the time the Moon has traveled those 670 miles, the Moon never gets any closer to Earth. It just keeps falling around Earth. As one astronomer has put it, the Moon stays up because it keeps falling down. Notice the pattern of orbital speeds of the planets in Question 37. The farther away from the Sun a planet is, the slower its orbital speed needs to be (see also Question 42).

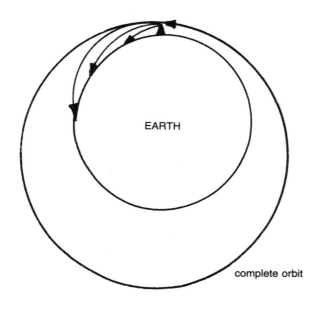

A supercannon (that is, a satellite launching rocket) gives its projectile enough speed to send it coasting around Earth without falling back to the surface. The three other projectiles fall to Earth's surface because they were not given enough speed.

42 Does a planet's orbit ever change?

A planet's orbit changes only by very small amounts as it exerts gravitational force on the other planets. A planet does not undergo large changes in its orbit unless some very massive outside force speeds up the planet or slows it down significantly. The same is true of the Moon and artificial satellites. For example, for an artificial satellite to remain in orbit 1,800 miles above Earth, it must have a speed of 14,670 miles an hour. If it is slowed down, it will begin to fall toward Earth. To settle into a new orbit at a lower altitude instead of continuing to fall toward the ground, the satellite must then be given more speed than it had in its higher orbit, since the gravitational attraction at the lower altitude is greater than at the higher altitude. For example, to remain in orbit at an altitude of 651 miles, the satellite must be given a speed of 16,396 miles an hour.

The orbits of the planets remain very much the same since there has not been any significant outside force to change their orbital speeds, at least none that we know of. But there could be. If an object with the mass of Jupiter, let's say, passed through the Solar System and came close to Mars, for instance, its gravitational attraction could whip Mars into a new orbit. This may actually have happened to one of the moons of Neptune. Some astronomers think that sometime in the past an invading object—possibly a tenth planet—swept in close to Neptune and gravitationally whipped away one of Neptune's moons, breaking it in two and putting it in a long, stretched-out orbit around the Sun. The snatched-away object became Pluto and its moon Charon.

Astronomers detect certain irregularities in the orbits of Uranus and Neptune, which suggests that some unseen object—maybe that tenth planet—is gravitationally disturbing those two planets from time to time (see Question 44).

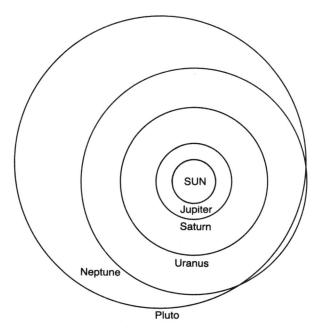

In 1979 Pluto crossed Neptune's orbit, which made Neptune the most distant planet rather than Pluto. In 1999 Pluto will recross the orbit of Neptune and once again be the most distant planet.

43 Why did Pluto cross Neptune's orbit?

Pluto, the end planet in the Solar System, has an unusual orbit. It is a long and stretched-out one (see Question 42) that sometimes causes Pluto to be closer to the Sun than Neptune. In 1979 Pluto crossed Neptune's orbit, which means that for a while Neptune will be the end planet. Pluto will recross Neptune's orbit in 1999 and once again be the most distant of the known planets. The orbits, however, are widely separated so there can never be a collision.

44 Why do the planets have gravity?

No one knows what *gravity* is, but the work of Sir Isaac Newton, in the 1600s, showed that gravity is a force that can be measured. Every object that exists has the force of gravity. That means that any two objects in space, no matter how distant, will attract each other—two golf balls, two elephants, two stars, or one star and its family of planets.

There are two important things about gravity: 1) The more massive two objects are, or the more matter packed into them, the greater their force of attraction for each other; and 2) The closer two objects are to each other, the greater their force of attraction. That means that Earth's gravitational tug on a low-flying satellite is stronger than it is on a high-flying satellite. And that means the low-flying satellite must have a greater speed than the high-flying one to remain in orbit (see Question 42). If we double the distance between two objects, gravitational attraction is not one-half what it was before, but only one-quarter. And the opposite is true. If we move two objects 10 times closer together than they were before, the force of gravitational attraction between them is not 10 times greater, but 100 times greater.

45 How much gravity do Jupiter and the Moon have?

The more mass, or matter, an object has, the greater its force of gravity. Your weight at the surface of any celestial body is the strength of the gravitational forces exerted by the body on you. Any object resting on Earth's surface is attracted to Earth's center, called the *center of mass*. While the Moon has only one-sixth the gravitational pulling force of Earth, the planet Jupiter has nearly three times as much. On the Moon you could jump six times higher than you can on Earth, and it would take six times longer for you to come back down to the ground again. On a small asteroid your weight would be even less, so you would have no trouble throwing a ball into orbit around the asteroid. On an even smaller asteroid—about a mile in diameter—you could jump off into orbit yourself.

The astronauts speak of "pulling *g*'s" when they reenter Earth's atmosphere from space. The air has a braking effect and slows down any object entering it from space. On returning from the Moon, the Apollo astronauts pulled about 7 *g*'s briefly. That means that they were being pushed down into their seats with seven times their weight on the ground. When you take off in a jet airliner, you are pushed back into your seat briefly with just a fraction of a *g*. Here are the values of gravity on the Sun and nine planets. To find your weight on the other planets, multiply your weight by the number in the "Gravity" column. (Notice that we are uncertain about Pluto's gravity, since that planet's great distance makes it difficult to measure.)

STRENGTH OF GRAVITY

Object	Gravity (times Earth's gravity)
Sun	27.8
Mercury	0.38
Venus	0.90
Earth	1.0
Moon	0.16
Mars	0.38
Asteroid Ceres	0.03
Jupiter	2.87
Saturn	1.32
Uranus	0.93
Neptune	1.23
Pluto	0.03(?)

46 What makes the astronauts float in the space shuttle?

A total lack of gravity or *g* force (see Question 45) is called *weightlessness* or *zero gravity*. The astronauts, whether on their way to the Moon or circling Earth in orbit aboard the space shuttle, are weightless. And so is their spacecraft. So any objects, including people, not fastened down float about in the cabin (see Question 47). Some of the astronauts have experienced space sickness, due to weightlessness. The feeling is like being seasick or airsick.

Other astronauts have not become sick. Most astronauts say that they enjoy being weightless.

47 How do astronauts eat in space?

During their journey to the Moon, the Apollo astronauts ate freeze-dried food packed in vacuum packages. All they had to do was add water and eat. To do this the astronaut fitted a nozzle to a valve on the food bag and added the amount of water called for. Next he squeezed the bag this way and that to mix the water and food. He then put the nozzle in his mouth and squeezed out the food. While eating in zero gravity (see Question 46), an astronaut must remember to keep his or her mouth closed to prevent pieces of food from escaping and floating around in the air. Biscuits and cookies could be a real crumb problem. To solve it, they are packaged in tasty wrappers and are eaten package and all. Since water doesn't pour in zero gravity, the astronauts must squeeze it into their mouths from packages.

48 Why do the astronauts have to wear special suits in space and on the Moon?

There is no air in space or on the Moon. Through the ages our bodies have adapted to nature's conditions on Earth's surface—temperature range, an atmosphere with about 20 percent oxygen, and an atmospheric pressure that pushes against every square inch of our bodies with a force of about 14 pounds.

Because there is no air in space, there is no oxygen to breathe. And because there is no atmospheric pressure, the body fluids of a person exposed in space would seep out through the skin and evaporate. A person adrift in space without protection against the lack of pressure would become completely dehydrated, like a dried prune. His or her body would be preserved there forever—a sort of space mummy. Space is bitter cold, since there is no atmosphere to transfer heat. There also is extremely damaging radiation, including ultraviolet and cosmic rays. The spacesuits worn by astronauts provide protection from such radiation, and provide heat, oxygen, and air pressure.

Conditions on the Moon are just as severe—no oxygen, no atmosphere, and exposure to radiation. A large temperature range is another condition that made it necessary for the Apollo astronauts to wear spacesuits when they walked on the Moon. By day the Moon's surface rocks heat up to about 200° F. By night the surface cools down to about −250° F.

49 Why do astronauts want to explore space?

The exploration of space is so costly that it can be done only by nations, not by individuals or even large corporations. The United States has several reasons for wanting to explore space—for military purposes, to demonstrate its technological achievement to the rest of the world, and for scientific purposes.

The National Academy of Science has established the search for life beyond Earth as a major goal of space biology. From a scientific point of view, the reason we are exploring space is a simple one: curiosity. We want to know about ourselves, how life arose on Earth, and how our planet and the Sun were formed. We also want to know if life has evolved elsewhere in the Solar System and in the Universe at large, or whether Earth is alone as an abode of life. These are not questions of the space age alone. People have been asking them for centuries. But only since the space age began has it become possible to find answers.

As individuals, the astronauts find space exploration extremely exciting. They regard their work as being patriotic and very important since they are helping to find answers to questions about the planets and stars that have been asked for centuries.

50 Why do spaceships split apart into different stages?

Consider a one-stage rocket with a full tank of fuel. The fuel is ignited, and the rocket climbs and reaches a speed of two miles a second. If it has enough fuel to last for two minutes, and if it keeps going at that speed, the rocket travels 240 miles.

Now imagine a two-stage rocket, meaning two identical rockets, one perched on top of the other and both with full tanks of fuel. The bottom stage is ignited, and the rocket climbs and reaches a speed of two miles a second. Just before the bottom rocket's fuel is used up at the end of two minutes, the fuel of the top stage part of the rocket is ignited. At the same time the spent bottom stage breaks away and falls back to Earth. The top stage, given a free ride by the bottom stage, has a speed of two miles a second when its fuel is ignited. It now reaches a new speed of four miles a second—two miles a second provided by the bottom stage plus another two miles a second provided by its own fuel. So in the first two minutes it travels 240 miles, and in the second two minutes, during its own burn, it travels 480 more miles, for a total of 720 miles.

In principle, that is how a multi-stage rocket works. In the example here the two-stage rocket actually would not travel 240 miles during the bottom-stage burn, since it has to carry the extra weight of the top stage. A rocket may have more than only two stages.

51 Why did it take so long for the Voyager spacecraft to get to Jupiter and Saturn?

Jupiter and Saturn are a great distance from us (see Question 34). Traveling at an average speed of about 31,000 miles an hour, it took *Voyager 1* a little more than three years (38 months) to reach Saturn from Earth, or a year and a half after it had explored Jupiter. It took longer for the spacecraft to get to Jupiter than it did for it to go from Jupiter to Saturn, which is about the same distance. The craft was speeded up by being whipped along by Jupiter's gravitation. At mission's end the little craft, about the size of a compact car, was less than 12 miles off course. This remarkable robot explorer had been programmed to correct its own navigation errors and even make its own repairs. Saturn's great distance from us becomes meaningful when we learn that the radio signals sent to *Voyager 1* by mission control at the Jet Propulsion Laboratory, in Pasadena, California, took an hour and 25 minutes to reach Saturn. Those signals traveled at the speed of light.

52 Why doesn't grass grow on the Moon?

In order for grass to grow, there must be water, temperatures above freezing but not too hot, and an atmosphere containing carbon dioxide and oxygen. The Moon (see Question 48) does not have water in its soil, the nighttime temperature plunges to $-250°$ F, while the day temperature rises to $200°$ F, and there is no atmosphere on the Moon.

53 Why can't sound travel through space?

Sound cannot travel through a vacuum, and since space is nearly a perfect vacuum, sound cannot travel through it. To talk to each other in space, or on the Moon, astronauts use radio. Radio waves can travel through a vacuum as well as through the air, just like light rays and X rays, for example. Here is how sound travels.

When you snap a tuning fork, you cause the two arms of the fork to vibrate back and forth rapidly. Each vibration pushes the air around the fork into a wave of tightly packed air particles (molecules). A train of such waves travels through the air as *sound waves*. When the waves strike our eardrum, the eardrum produces vibrations of its own, which the ear "hears" as sound. Much the same thing happens in the water when you click two rocks together, or through a metal rod when you tap one end with a hammer.

54 Why is the sky blue, and why is it black out in space?

As light from the Sun shines down through Earth's atmosphere the light strikes the many air molecules and is *scattered*. Because the blue wavelengths of light are scattered more than the wavelengths of other colors, the sky appears blue. Scattering occurs because the air molecules are small compared with the wavelengths of blue light. The atmosphere becomes less and less dense higher above Earth's surface. This means that there are fewer air molecules high up in the atmosphere than there are at lower altitudes, so the sky up there is a much darker blue. At still higher altitudes there are so few air molecules that there is no scattering, so the sky is black. And that is why the sky is black in space.

55 Why isn't there any water on any of the other planets?

Earth's water is kept circulating through the *hydrologic cycle*: Ocean water evaporates and enters the atmosphere as the gas water vapor, which forms clouds, cools, and falls as rain. The rain water flows back to the sea again as rivers and streams, so completing the cycle.

Mercury and the Moon lack atmospheres, so they cannot have hydrologic cycles. Further, their sunlit surfaces are too hot, and their shaded surfaces are too cold, to support pools of liquid water. Venus's surface is too hot (860° F) all over to support liquid water. Mars has a very thin atmosphere with hardly any water vapor. But early in its history the planet probably had a dense atmosphere with lots of water vapor. We can imagine a time when torrential rains pelted Mars. The marks left by the raging rivers would have stayed on the surface long after the planet entered its present ice age as its atmosphere dried out and thinned to its present state. The small summer patch of Mars's northern hemisphere polar ice cap seems to be mostly water ice. Almost all of Mars's water supply is locked up as polar cap ice and in the ground. If it could all be released and changed to liquid water, there would be only enough to form a small pond.

The giant planets—Jupiter, Saturn, Uranus, and Neptune—have dense atmospheres composed mostly of the gas hydrogen. While they probably have planet-wide oceans of liquid hydrogen more than a thousand miles deep, they cannot have bodies of liquid water. Jupiter's moons Callisto, Ganymede, and Europa all have surfaces made of water ice. The ice plates of Europa's crust may be floating on a sea of liquid water that covers a rock-metal core. Saturn's moons also seem to be coated with water ice. We know very little about the moons of Uranus and Neptune. Pluto probably is an icy little world, but its ice is the frozen gas methane, not water.

56 *What are the planets made of?*

We can group the planets into two divisions—the *terrestrial* planets and the *giant* planets. The *terrestrial* planets are Mercury, Venus, Earth, and Mars. All have hard crusts composed of lightweight silicate rocks. Beneath the crust is a thick layer of heavier-weight rock. And forming the core of each planet is an immense ball of metal. The cores of Mercury, Venus, and Earth are composed of iron and nickel. The core of Mars may be a combination of iron and sulfur.

The giant planets are Jupiter, Saturn, Uranus, and Neptune. All four are similar, although not exactly alike. All have upper atmospheres mostly of the gas hydrogen along with some helium. The cloud-top temperatures are colder than $-400°$ F. Because the pressure increases with depth into each planet, the temperatures also increase. At a depth of several hundred miles, the hydrogen gas turns into a deep layer of hydrogen slush, beneath which is a deep layer of liquid hydrogen. At the core of each of the giants there may be a ball of rocky material several thousands of degrees hot.

57 Why don't all the planets have air like Earth's?

Each planet's distance from the Sun (see Question 34) is one reason for a planet having the kind of air it has. The planet's geological history is another reason. Mercury does not have an atmosphere, and it is unlikely that it ever did have one. The planet's low surface gravity (see Question 45) was too weak to hold on to the gases that bubbled up out of the interior when Mercury was young. Venus, nearly as massive as Earth, did hold on to its atmosphere. It is nothing like Earth's. Venus's upper clouds are not made of water droplets as Earth's clouds are. Instead, they are clouds of sulfuric acid. Venus's air is extremely dense, so dense that objects more than 300 feet away would appear blurred. Atmospheric pressure at the surface is 90 times more than on Earth. Venus's surface winds are more like a river current than a breeze. The air is 97 percent carbon dioxide and 3 percent nitrogen. Venus's closeness to the Sun may have heated the planet so much that large amounts of carbon dioxide locked up in Venus's rocks were released and collected in the atmosphere.

The low surface gravity of Mars was too weak to hold on to the planet's original atmosphere. Gradually the lightweight gases escaped from the planet, leaving mostly the heavy gas carbon dioxide, which makes up about 70 percent of the Martian air today. The other 30 percent is argon.

The atmospheres of the giant planets Jupiter, Saturn, Uranus, and Neptune are mostly hydrogen, along with some helium. There are lesser amounts of methane, ammonia, and other gases. Because the gas giant planets are so massive, their surface gravity is high. This means that they were able to retain large amounts of the original gases contained in the solar nebula out of which the planets were formed (see Question 23).

58 Why are the planets round?

Planets and stars are round, or sphere shaped, for the same reason. A star forms out of a huge cloud of gas and dust (see Question 25). The denser regions of such a cloud gravitationally attract surrounding matter. Eventually there is a superdense patch of matter that then attracts the remaining surrounding matter into itself. All of the matter is attracted inward toward the densest part of the globe, the center of mass (see Question 45). Since all of the matter is pulled toward a common point, the star or planet takes the shape of a sphere.

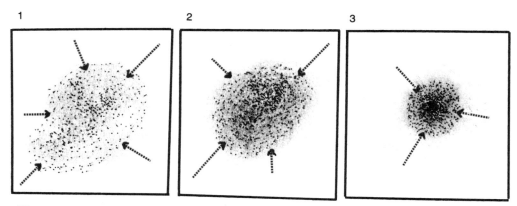

When a celestial cloud of gas, dust, and heavier clumps of matter forms, it collapses in on itself toward the center of mass of the cloud. In this way the matter packs itself around the dense central region and gradually shapes itself as a sphere. That is why stars and planets are shaped as spheres.

59 How did the planets get their names?

Many centuries ago when astronomy was a young science in Greece, people associated the Sun, Moon, and planets with their various gods, and so named the planets. When the Romans conquered the Greeks in war, the Romans substituted the names of their gods, and those are the names we use today.

Because they did not understand the world in a scientific way, the Greeks believed that the Sun, Moon, and planets were associated with gods, or *were* gods. The Sun was associated with life and energy and given the name Helios, who in mythology drove a chariot across the heavens. Because Mercury was seen to move swiftly, the planet was named after the fleet-footed messenger of the gods, Hermes. Venus was regarded as an object of beauty since that planet was the brightest object in the sky, other than the Sun and Moon, so it was named after the beautiful goddess of love, Aphrodite. Mars was seen as a red object and associated with blood and war, so was named after the god of war, Ares. Jupiter, the largest planet, was appropriately named after the king of the gods, Zeus. And Saturn, which was seen to move so slowly, was named after the god of time, Kronos.

The other planets were not discovered until after the telescope came into use in 1609. Sir William Herschel discovered Uranus in the year 1781. He wanted to name the planet Georgium Sidus, after England's King George III. Others began calling the planet Herschel. But some astronomers said that any new planets should be named after Roman gods to keep the system of names consistent. So Uranus, the father of Saturn and grandfather of Jupiter, was selected as the name for Herschel's planet. Neptune, discovered in 1846, was named after the Roman god of the sea. Pluto, far from the Sun and barely visible, was named after the Roman god of the underworld. Pluto's moon, Charon, was named after the figure in Roman mythology who operated the ferryboat that carried the souls of the dead across the River Styx into the underworld.

It has been agreed by an international association of astronomers, the

International Astronomical Union, that any new planets will be named after Roman gods. The only exceptions to this rule are the known moons of Uranus—Ariel, Umbriel, Titania, and Oberon. Those names come from characters named by William Shakespeare and Alexander Pope. Comets are the only celestial bodies named after the person who discovered the comet. Halley's Comet, for example, was named after the English astronomer Edmond Halley.

60 What makes Earth and the other planets spin, and why don't we fall off?

Earth and the other planets were formed some 4.6 billion years ago out of clouds of matter contained in the disk region of the solar gas and dust cloud (see Question 23). Each newly forming planet attracted surrounding matter into itself by gravitation. Gravity also caused this newly swept-up matter to contract tightly around the core region. Contraction caused the planet to start spinning, and the greater the contraction, the faster the spinning became. You have seen the effect if you have ever watched a figure skater start spinning in place. The skater begins spinning slowly at first, but then pulls his or her arms in closer to the body (contraction), which makes the spin faster. This is how stars, as well as planets, are set spinning when they form. The spinning is called *rotational velocity*.

All objects at Earth's surface are attracted toward the center of the planet by gravitation (see Question 45). Even though a person standing at the equator is being spun around at the speed of 1,000 miles an hour, gravity holds the person firmly in place. Since they could not *feel* Earth rotating, before about 1600 people refused to believe that Earth rotated. They argued that if it did, birds would be whipped off their perches. Other people refused to believe that Earth was round. They argued that if it were, people living at the bottom of Earth would fall off.

Following are the rates of rotation of the Sun and planets:

RATES OF ROTATION OF THE SUN AND ITS PLANETS

Object	Rotation
Sun	27 Earth days (at equator)
Mercury	59 Earth days
Venus	243 Earth days (rotates backward)
Earth	23 hours 56 minutes
Mars	24 hours 37 minutes
Jupiter	9 hours 55 minutes
Saturn	10 hours 40 minutes
Uranus	13 hours 24 minutes (?) (rotates backward)
Neptune	18 hours 30 minutes (?)
Pluto	6 days 9 hours (rotates backward)

61 How did Jupiter and Saturn get their rings, and why don't the rings go away?

Voyager 1 discovered that Jupiter has a ring. Like dust grains glimmering in a beam of light, the ring particles of Jupiter are fine and faint. The ring seems to be less than a mile or so thick, but stretches out from Jupiter's upper cloud deck to a distance of 36,000 miles. We do not know what the ring particles are made of. They may be volcanic ash captured from Jupiter's volcanically active moon, Io. They may be meteoroid and comet dust, or debris from Jupiter's fourteenth moon, which seems to be breaking up as it orbits Jupiter at the ring's edge. So Jupiter appears to have a source of material (Io and its fourteenth moon) to supply its ring with debris.

Saturn's splendid ring system has been known since the early 1600s. The seven major rings extend outward from the planet for more than 43,000 miles but are only a little more than a half-mile thick. This is the equivalent of a phonograph record three miles in diameter. How Saturn's rings were formed is as much of a mystery today as it was a century ago. The particles are lumps of ice mixed with dust. They range in size from tiny dust grains to lumps the size of a railroad freight car. The larger ring fragments seem to collide and so break down into smaller particles. Many astronomers think that the ring particles are matter left over from the time Saturn was formed. But other scientists have wondered whether the ring particles are the remains of a moon that wandered in too close to Saturn and was torn apart by the planet's gravitation. The ring system is not one continuous ring but a series of perhaps a thousand individual ringlets. The gravitational attraction of Saturn's moons as they circle the planet at different speeds seems to keep the ring system "fenced in." Without the moons, the ring particles might scatter and be lost to space.

62 Why are some planets big and others small?

When the Sun and planets were being formed (see Questions 23 and 25) the cloud of gas and dust out of which the Sun formed extended out between

Jupiter's Great Red Spot as photographed by the 200-inch telescope. (Hale Observatories)

Mars and the asteroid belt (see Question 4). Meanwhile, the planets were forming out of smaller globes of matter embedded in the disk matter spun off by the rotating cloud of Sun material. At this stage all of the planets may have been about the same size. But then the cloud of Sun matter collapsed in on itself. As it did, the outer regions rushed inward as a strong wind that swept past Mars, Earth, Venus, and Mercury. In the process those terrestrial planets were robbed of much of their matter. The outer giant planets were not affected since they were outside the cloud of Sun material. That is how some astronomers think that the terrestrial planets failed to acquire the mass and size of the giants Jupiter, Saturn, Uranus, and Neptune.

63 What is the Great Red Spot on Jupiter?

The most prominent feature of Jupiter's atmosphere is its Great Red Spot, a gigantic football-shaped blob of gases, twice Earth's size, that floats in the planet's southern hemisphere near the equator. First observed in the late 1600s, the Great Red Spot has persisted over the centuries, changing from time to time from a bright red to a dull brick red, and back to bright red again. The spot rotates and seems to be an enormous high-pressure system.

64 Since there is lightning in Jupiter's upper clouds, and the clouds are made of hydrogen, why doesn't Jupiter explode?

In Earth's atmosphere a balloon of hydrogen gas struck by lightning would explode, or burn violently. It would burn because it would combine with oxygen in the air. Burning, or *combustion*, is defined as rapid oxidation, meaning a rapid combining with oxygen. Since Jupiter's clouds lack oxygen, combustion cannot take place there.

65 Why is Pluto so small?

Pluto probably isn't a real planet at all. Instead, it may be an escaped moon of Neptune. Some astronomers suspect that a tenth planet, or some other object, swept in close to Neptune and its moons. As it did, its gravitational tug whipped one of Neptune's moons out of orbit and broke it in two. Both entered a new orbit around the Sun. The larger object became Pluto and the smaller chip became Pluto's moon, Charon. No one knows if that is really how Pluto came to be.

66 Why are the planets different colors?

Mercury and the Moon appear gray generally because that is the color of their surface rocks. Since neither Mercury nor the Moon has an atmosphere, we have taken very clear photographs of their surfaces. Venus is ever wrapped in a dense layer of clouds, the tops of which contain sulfur and certain other substances that give the clouds a slight yellowish color. Earth, the blue planet, gets its bluish color from the scattering of light (see Question 54). Mars, nicknamed the ''Red Planet,'' gets its reddish color from its sprawling deserts, which contain large amounts of rusty sand and dust. This rusty substance is iron oxide.

Jupiter and Saturn are enclosed beneath a dense cloud layer hundreds of miles deep. Jupiter's clouds are heavily banded with white, dull red, and brownish red stripes girdling the planet. The bands dissolve, re-form, and have swirls and loops between them. Saturn's clouds also are banded but lack the rich and varied colors of Jupiter. Saturn's cloud tops glow a pale

Like the Moon, Mercury lacks an atmosphere and appears as a grayish world pockmarked by thousands of craters. Certain chemicals in the cloud tops of the giant planets and Venus give those planets their familiar colors. This composite photograph of Mercury was taken in 1974 by Mariner 10. (NASA)

yellow, muted by a haze of hydrogen enclosing the planet. Saturn's atmosphere has a reddish oval structure more than 6,000 miles long and located in the Southern Hemisphere. It may be similar to Jupiter's Great Red Spot (see Question 63).

Uranus glows with a dim greenish color, which suggests that the planet's atmosphere contains the gas methane, in addition to mostly hydrogen along with some helium. Neptune and Uranus can be thought of as twin planets in size and structure. But Neptune's cloud tops glow with a pale bluish light.

67 Why is Venus's sky red instead of blue?

Earth's sky appears blue (see Question 54) because the air molecules scatter blue light, or shortwave radiation, more than they scatter longer-wave radiation, such as red light. So on Earth blue light reaches us from all directions. The extremely dense air at Venus's surface (see Question 69) scatters all colors of light, except red, so much that our vision would be best down in the red region of the color spectrum. So Venus's sky would appear red rather than blue.

68 Why is Venus's surface hot enough to melt lead?

Venus's closeness to the Sun may have heated up the planet so much that large amounts of carbon dioxide locked up in Venus's rocks were released and collected in the atmosphere. The carbon dioxide then acted as a heat trap, in what is called the *greenhouse effect*. Shortwave radiation from the Sun penetrates Venus's clouds and heats up the ground. The ground then gives off heat in the form of long-wave radiation. This long-wave radiation cannot pass up through the carbon dioxide "blanket" enclosing Venus. So it is trapped as heat and keeps Venus's surface region at a temperature of 860° F, hot enough to melt lead.

69 What kind of air does Venus have?

For many years astronomers tended to look on Venus as Earth's twin planet. But in recent years, satellite studies of Venus's atmosphere, for example, reveal Venus as a very untwinly "twin." Venus's cloud tops are about 45 miles above the planet's surface (compared with Earth's, which are about 50 or so miles above its surface) and are swept around Venus once every four days by strong winds blowing about 220 miles an hour. The clouds are not made of water droplets, as Earth's clouds are. Instead, they are clouds of sulfuric acid. At an altitude of about 30 miles, the clouds thin, and the air is clear from there down to the surface. The winds slow, although still blowing steadily westward, to 110 miles an hour, and they slow even more at lower altitudes. The *Pioneer Venus 2* space probe found that Venus has 3 times more krypton and 75 times more argon than Earth's air does. Venus's air is about 97 percent carbon dioxide (compared with Earth's less than 1 percent) and about 3 percent nitrogen (compared with Earth's 78 percent). The atmospheric pressure at Venus's surface is 90 times that on Earth, enough to crush you to death. And the air temperature is 860° F, enough to bake you. The air is so dense that a gentle breeze on Venus would carry you along like a river current would. Also, this superdense air makes Venus's sky appear red instead of blue (see Question 67).

70 Are there other planets that we don't know of?

Most astronomers would answer that there must be planets we don't know of. When stars form out of immense clouds of gas and dust (see Question 92) planets probably form right along with them. There are more than 500 billion stars in our galaxy alone, and there are billions of other galaxies. If only one out of 10 of our galaxy's stars have planets, that would amount to 50 billion stars with planets. And if the average number of planets per star was, say, five, then there would be 250 billion planets in the Milky Way galaxy.

Astronomers have studied many stars in hopes of finding evidence for other planetary systems. But the stars are so very far away that our Earth-bound telescopes cannot see planets of stars other than the Sun. A star called Barnard's star wobbles a bit, which makes some astronomers suspect that the star may have an unseen planet, about the mass of Jupiter, revolving about it. More recently, a space telescope that "sees" in infrared light has detected cloudy matter surrounding the star Vega. The cloud extends outward from Vega to a distance of about 15 billion miles. The cloud matter may contain planets, or it may be material out of which planets are now being formed. Vega is in the constellation Lyra and lies at a distance of some 150 trillion miles from the Sun. Astronomers also have detected an object, associated with the star T Tauri in the constellation Taurus, that may be a planet now being formed. It appears to be about 20 times more massive than Jupiter. T Tauri is about 2,700 trillion miles away.

71 Is there a tenth planet in the Solar System? and Why are there only nine planets?

There may be one or several more planets beyond Pluto, but our most powerful telescopes have not spotted any.

As Uranus moves in its orbit, it does not move "smoothly" as we would expect it to. It speeds up and slows down now and then. This suggests that there may be an object far beyond Pluto gravitationally influencing the orbital motion of Neptune (see Question 42). Irregular motions of Uranus for the same reason led to the discovery of Neptune in the year 1846. Then after Uranus passed Neptune, Neptune tended to hold Uranus back and so slowed it down.

In 1977 the astronomer Charles Kowal discovered a mysterious object lying out beyond Saturn. At first he wondered if it could be a tenth planet. The object turned out to be a little world smaller than Earth. It was named Chiron. Like the major planets, it circles the Sun and so technically can be called a planet, or an asteroid.

72 Is there life on other planets?

The Viking spacecraft that landed on Mars and conducted chemical experiments with the Martian soil failed to convince biologists that Mars supports any form of life whatever; but maybe it does. And possibly simple life forms, such as bacteria, exist deep down in the warm layers of Jupiter's clouds, or in clouds of the other giant planets. We can be certain that advanced life forms, such as mammals, do not exist on any other planet in the Solar System because conditions there are too harsh, except possibly in the water of Jupiter's moon Europa (see Question 57).

But this does not rule out advanced life forms on planets of other star systems in our galaxy. Many astronomers feel that there is a good possibility that hundreds of millions of stars in our home galaxy have conditions favorable enough to support advanced forms of life. By "advanced" is meant intelligent beings capable of developing a technology at least as advanced as our own; and by "favorable" is meant climate, atmosphere and atmospheric pressure, and so on, that we ourselves would describe as "comfortable." To be habitable, a planet must not be too close to its local star because it would be too hot (like Mercury) to support life. And the planet must not be too far away, or it would be too cold (like Pluto) to support life. Further, a habitable planet's air and atmospheric pressure must be just right for life to form and flourish. On the whole, scientists see no reason to suppose that of the trillions of stars known to exist, the Sun should be the only star with a planet suitable for life.

73 Why don't people live on other planets?

Intelligent beings, although not ''people'' like us, most likely do inhabit planets belonging to other stars in our home galaxy, and in other galaxies beyond (see Question 72). The question might have been, ''Why haven't we moved to other planets to live on them?'' Our technology could soon make it possible for a colony of several thousand humans to cross space and take up life on other planets. Our first step in this direction was to land astronauts on the Moon. The second step would be to build a space settlement in permanent orbit about Earth. Such a settlement would be home for 10,000 or so people. The third step could be for a smaller such colony to journey to one or more stars in search of habitable planets. Such a journey might take several generations. So some of these space explorers would be born in the journeying colony and spend their entire lives in it before the mission was complete.

74 Why don't the artificial satellites in space burn up?

Any artificial satellite in a stable orbit around Earth will not burn up because it is above the planet's dense atmosphere. Skylab and other artificial satellites have burned up because their orbits decreased. This caused the satellites to graze the top of the atmosphere. Drag, or friction, against the air slowed down the satellite a bit more each time it orbited Earth and cut a little deeper into the atmosphere. Eventually the air put the brakes on so much that the satellite's orbit took it down toward the ground (see Question 41), and as it sped through the dense air it heated up so much that it burned up, just as a meteoroid is burned up when we see it as a meteor (see Question 4).

75 How many spaceships have we (U.S.A.) sent up? How many have all the countries together sent up?

As this book is being written, there are 4,914 satellite objects orbiting Earth. About four-fifths of those objects are space "junk," rocket bodies, nose cones, and spent fuel containers, for example. The total number of satellite objects shot into space since the first satellite, *Sputnik 1,* launched by the Russians in 1957, is 14,000. Two-thirds of them have since fallen back to Earth.

Of the 4,914 objects currently in orbit, about 290 are actively doing something. Of those 290, about 180 are owned by the United States. About 100 belong to Russia, Japan, Canada, Indonesia, India, China, and Australia. The rest are owned by European nations.

Among the tasks performed by the satellites are: geological surveying, relaying communications, weather watch service, spying, and photographing everything and anything visible.

ARTIFICIAL SATELLITE SCOREBOARD

Number Launched	Number Still Operating
2,069 (Soviet Union)	102
997 (United States)	183
59 (other nations)	7

76 How big is the Solar System?

The most distant planet in the Solar System is Pluto, lying at a distance of some 3.6 billion miles from the Sun (see Question 34). So double that distance, or 7.2 billion miles, would be the diameter of the Solar System if we use Pluto as the most distant object. But the comets also are members of the Solar System, and they lie at a much greater distance from the Sun than Pluto does. The comets seem to occupy a huge volume of space called the Oort cloud (see Question 1). The edge of the sphere is thought to lie some 140 trillion miles from the Sun. So if we use the comets as the most distant members of the Solar System, then its diameter is nearly 280 trillion miles.

77 How were all the moons made?

About 4.6 billion years ago, the Sun, the planets and moons, and the comets were formed out of a huge cloud of gas and dust (see Question 23). Most of the gas was hydrogen, along with some helium, and relatively small amounts of all the other elements. As the great cloud of matter contracted under the influence of gravitation (see Question 58), it began spinning, and it cast off matter that formed a huge spinning disk extending outward from the central mass of the cloud. Globes of matter formed within the disk material and became the planets. There also was a smaller disk of matter flung out from each rotating planet globe. The moons of the planets then formed out of the planet-disk material.

78 Why does Jupiter have the most moons?

Jupiter does not have the greatest number of moons. Saturn does. At latest count Saturn has 22 moons. Jupiter has 17. We would expect the giant planets to have more moons than the smaller, terrestrial planets. Why? Because when the planets were formed the terrestrial planets (Mercury, Venus, Earth, and Mars) were robbed of some of their matter when the solar gas cloud collapsed (see Question 62). Because the gas giant planets (Jupiter, Saturn, Uranus, and Neptune) were not robbed of material by the great collapse, they had more matter out of which moons could be formed (see Question 77). Also, astronomers think that some of the smaller moons of massive Jupiter are captured asteroids rather than moons that formed originally out of Jupiter's disk matter.

79 Why do craters on the Moon look like a face?

The Moon's surface features—craters and maria (see Questions 16, 17, and 18)—can appear to our mind's eye as just about any shape we want to give them. They are especially suggestive of distinctive shapes when the Moon is a crescent shape or a half moon. At such times the shadow line running down across the Moon outlines mountains and cuts across craters and the maria. As we gaze at the Moon at such times, our imaginations can ''see'' various shapes, the ''man in the Moon'' being one. Perhaps you have watched fluffy clouds change their shapes on a lazy summer afternoon and imagined them to form a face, an elephant, or some other figure. While you could make out a face, for instance, perhaps someone else watching with you saw a fish instead. Stargazers of old imagined various figures making up those star groups we call the constellations (see Question 9). A friend of mine recently said, ''I finally saw the 'man in the Moon.' It took a rising full moon and naked eyes. He was smiling broadly at me.''

80 Can Earth have lots of explosions like the Sun?

No. The Sun is an extremely active object, a ball of hot gases producing enormous amounts of energy in its core region (see Question 26). As this energy flows up to the Sun's surface, great fiery loops of gases erupt out of the Sun's surface. There also are sunspots (see Question 35), which are great magnetic storms that boil up out of the Sun's surface gases. Earth is a solid object that does not produce energy of its own making, so it has no way of exploding or sending out great outbursts of energy as the Sun does.

But Earth does go through periods of local eruptions in the form of volcanoes. And there are earthquakes. Earthquakes are caused when great crustal plates of rock move about and the edges grind against each other. When two plates pressing and rubbing against each other (like your thumb and finger pressing against each other and then snapping) snap free, there is an earthquake. Volcanoes erupt when molten rock in pools beneath the rock crust melts its way up through cracks in the crustal rock and spills out as lava.

81 Do any of the other planets have volcanoes, or is Earth the only one?

Earth is not the only one. Venus has what may be one of the Solar System's largest canyons. It is nearly four times longer than our Grand Canyon and about twice as deep. Geologists think that in ages past, Venus's crust split open and so formed the canyon. Venusquakes may be common in the canyon area now, and huge outpourings of molten rock may well up and spread out onto the canyon floor from time to time. Lava lakes of molten rock may be common in this region.

Although Mars seems not to have active volcanoes now, it certainly did in the past. A region called Tharsis is the site of four enormous volcanoes. The giant among them is Olympus Mons, three times larger than Earth's largest volcano, Mauna Loa, and three times as high as Mount Everest. Volcanoes also are found in Mars's southern hemisphere, but not as many as in the north. Some of these volcanoes have impact crater scars on their slopes. This shows that the volcanoes are very old and existed when Mars was a young planet undergoing heavy asteroid bombardment (see Question 16).

Jupiter's moon Io is the most geologically active body among the planets. *Voyager 1* photographed 10 erupting volcanoes when it flew past Io in 1979. Enough matter is ejected out of Io's volcanoes to resurface that moon once every million years. Io's volcanoes may provide the material forming Jupiter's ring. The volcanoes spout streams of foul-smelling sulfur snow that provides Io with an ever-changing landscape. The black spot photographed by *Voyager 1* may be a dried-up lava bed. The orange red areas are sulfur deposits, some hot enough to be molten. We know of no other moons or planets that have active volcanoes, except for Venus, quite likely.

The giant Martian volcano Olympus Mons, as envisioned by an artist in a painting based on photos taken by the Viking space probe. The mountain is three times larger than Earth's largest volcano and three times higher than Earth's highest mountain. (NASA)

The light dome at top left is a large volcano erupting on the surface of Jupiter's moon Io. It was photo-graphed by Voyager 1 on March 4, 1979 from a distance of about 300,000 miles. (NASA)

82 About how much longer will Earth exist?

For nearly 5 billion years. To the best of our knowledge, the Sun, Earth, and the other planets were formed about 4.6 billion years ago (see Questions 23 and 25). Also to the best of our knowledge, the Sun is about halfway through its "life cycle," which means that it has about another 5 billion years to shine the way it shines today. But there must come a time when the Sun runs out of hydrogen fuel (see Question 26) to keep it shining, or pouring out energy that enables Earth to support life. When the Sun runs out of hydrogen fuel, its hot core region will cool. The Sun will then collapse in on itself and become a star called a red giant (see Question 29). When that happens, the Sun will swell up and engulf Mercury. It will give off so much energy so close to Earth that Earth's oceans will boil away and the surface will become so hot that the rock crust will melt. There will be nothing left of Earth except a soupy mass of bubbling rock.

After millions of years the Sun will shrink and cool to a tiny star called a white dwarf. It will then give off too little energy to warm its family of planets. Gradually the Sun will cool until it stops shining and becomes a dead star called a black dwarf. Earth and the other planets will then be cold, dark worlds.

83 What makes an eclipse?

An *eclipse* is the partial or total blocking from view of one celestial object by another's passing in front of it. A *lunar* eclipse occurs when the Moon passes through Earth's shadow. A *partial solar* eclipse occurs when the Moon

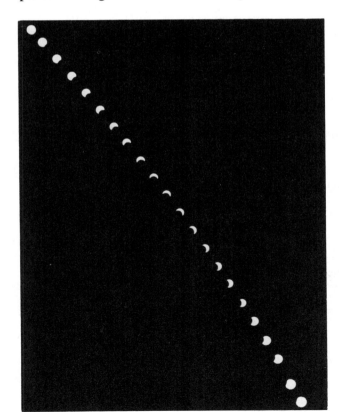

A partial solar eclipse photographed at six-minute intervals from Washington, D.C. on July 10, 1972. (NASA)

blocks only part of the Sun from view. In a *total solar* eclipse, the Moon completely covers the Sun's disk. An *annular solar* eclipse occurs when the Moon is centered on the Sun's disk but, because the Moon is at its greatest distance from Earth, it does not appear quite so large as the Sun and so leaves a narrow rim of the Sun visible.

84 What's a nebula?

A *nebula* is a great cloud of dust and gas within a galaxy. Some nebulae, said to be *reflection* nebulae, reflect light generated by nearby stars, or by stars embedded within the nebula. Other nebulae are dark and so are called *dark* nebulae. Still others reradiate energy emitted by stars embedded in the nebulae and are called *emission* nebulae. And still others take the form of a great shell of gas cast off by an eruptive, or explosive, star. These are called *planetary* nebulae because they were once mistaken for planets within the Solar System. There also are supernova remains (see Question 88).

85 Why can't a balloon go to the Moon?

A balloon rises through the air because the gas filling its bag is less dense, or lighter, than the surrounding air. Hydrogen and helium are the two lightest elements, and either can be used to float a balloon. If you hold a piece of wood under water and then let it go, the wood rises through the water and floats to the surface. This happens because the wood is less dense than the water. If you release a balloon into the air, the balloon rises through the air and keeps rising until the air around it is the same density as the gas in the balloon. The balloon will then float, neither rising nor sinking. Since there is a top to the atmosphere, and no air in space between Earth and the Moon, a balloon could not rise above the top of the atmosphere any more than the piece of wood floating in the water could rise into the air.

86 What are the Northern Lights?

Storms on the Sun cast off streams of charged atomic particles that sweep through the Solar System. The particles are electrons and protons. On reaching Earth, these charged particles are deflected by Earth's magnetism to the north and south magnetic poles, where they excite the atmosphere due to their collisions. We see the results as the *Northern Lights,* also called the *northern dawn* and *aurora borealis*. They are best seen from high latitudes, for example, from Canada. Photographs of the aurora show that it extends for a few hundred miles above Earth's surface, below the altitude of the space shuttle orbits.

Following is one kind of Northern Lights display. They may appear dimly at dusk and then for several hours blend into different glowing colors and weave graceful forms. When they first appear they color the graying sky with a yellowish or greenish white light in the form of a great arc. For a few hours the arc may change little, slowly falling off toward the south. Then quite suddenly the lower edge grows intense and sharp, and the arc separates into fanlike rays that blaze into pink, purple, and red. Parts of it may take on the form of pastel cosmic draperies — quivering, folding, and unfolding. This part of the show, when the aurora fills the entire northern sky, is the climax, but lasts only a few minutes. Gradually the forms dissolve, the intense colors fade, and the sky is left with a faint, glowing light. Although the Northern Lights may be seen now and then throughout the year, they are especially prominent and frequent during that part of the solar cycle when the Sun is active, building to an active stage once about every 11 years. The last period of the active Sun was around 1979, so the next period should be around 1990.

87 What causes the tides?

The rise and fall each day of Earth's oceans are caused by gravitational attraction of the Moon and Sun. If the Moon stayed motionless over the Pacific Ocean, a great bulge of water would pile up there. But because the Moon moves around Earth, it pulls the bulge of water along behind it. And because Earth turns about 30 times faster, it drags the bulge along ahead of the Moon. When the bulge approaches the shore, we say that we have a *high* tide; and when the bulge is pulled away from the shore we say that we have a *low* tide. Because of its greater distance from us, the Sun's ability to raise tides is only one-third that of the Moon's (see Question 44).

When the Sun and Moon are at right angles to one another we have *neap* tides. These are relatively weak tides because the Sun and Moon are attracting Earth's ocean water from two different directions. We have neap tides whenever the Moon is in first quarter or in last quarter.

When the Sun, Moon, and Earth are lined up, at new moon and full moon, we have relatively high tides called *spring* tides, which have nothing to do with the spring season. These tides are high because gravitational attractions

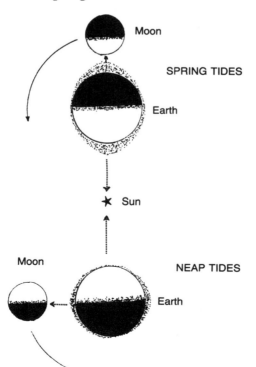

When the Sun, Earth, and Moon are in a straight line (top), the combined gravitational attraction of the Sun and Moon raise higher than normal tides on Earth, called spring tides. When the Sun and Moon are at right angles to each other with respect to Earth (bottom), the gravitational attraction of each is somewhat weakened and we have tides somewhat shallower than normal, called neap tides.

The Crab Nebula is the gaseous remains of a star that exploded in the year 1054 and is an example of a supernova explosion. (Hale Observatories)

of the Sun and Moon are acting in the same direction rather than in two different directions, as at neap tide.

88 What's a supernova, and a nova?

Blue giant stars, such as Rigel and Deneb, are extremely massive stars that may evolve into an explosive star called a *supernova*. Such stars become extremely unstable when they use up the last of their hydrogen fuel (see Question 27) and explode violently. They flare up and become thousands of times brighter than before. In a single second a supernova gives off as much energy as the Sun does in 60 years. The supernova of the year 1572 was so bright it could be seen in the daytime. In the year 1054, Chinese astronomers observed a supernova explosion, the remains of which we see as the Crab Nebula. The nebula is a great cloud of cast-off matter about 42 light-years across and expanding at a rate of about 800 miles per second. At the center of the nebula we can see the exposed core of the star that exploded, a small and extremely hot and bright object called a *neutron star* (see Question 89).

We know of fewer than a half dozen supernovae in our galaxy, but over the past 90 or so years more than 400 supernova stars have been observed in galaxies other than our own.

Nova stars are lesser versions of supernova stars. They flare up suddenly and mysteriously, increasing in brightness over a period of days or several weeks. Within a few days a typical nova may become 60,000 times brighter than usual, then it becomes somewhat less brilliant, and after a few months or longer returns to normal. Perhaps all novae are double star systems, one companion being a white dwarf. The brighter star transfers matter (hydrogen) to the white dwarf. When enough matter piles up on the surface of the white dwarf it explodes into helium. The result is a burst of light. Possibly 50 or so nova stars flare up in our galaxy every year.

89 Why do stars blow up?

The most massive stars, those tens of times more massive than the Sun, are the best candidates for explosion. But stars with the Sun's mass also are destined to swell up into red giant stars (see Question 82). In general, stars explode when they use up the last of their hydrogen fuel. When that happens, the star's energy production in the core lessens. The core region then cools a bit. With the cooling there is a drop in pressure in the core. So now there is not enough pressure in the core to prevent the surrounding gases from tumbling into the core region. The result is a great collapse of matter into the core. This sends the temperature and pressure soaring, resulting in a tremendous explosion.

90 What's a dwarf star?

There are three main classes of dwarf stars. White dwarfs are intensely bright and massive but small objects (see Question 29). For example, one white dwarf known as Kuiper's Star is as massive as the Sun but is only about the size of Mars. A thimbleful of its material weighed on Earth would weigh many tons. Stars nearing the end of their lives and swelling up as red giants (see Question 29), end their lives by shrinking and shining for billions of years as white dwarfs. Their hydrogen fuel supply spent, they are no longer able to produce new stores of energy in their core region. Gradually they grow dimmer and dimmer until eventually they cool as objects best described as black dwarfs.

Stars that do not become very massive when they are formed become stars known as *red dwarfs*. Their core temperatures are barely high enough (about 10 million degrees) to fuse hydrogen into helium and so shine by nuclear fusion (see Question 26). Such stars are only about a tenth as massive as the Sun. And because their surface temperature is only about 3,000 degrees Kelvin (compared with 6,000 degrees for the Sun), they shine with red light. The hotter Sun shines with a yellowish white light. The still hotter blue giant stars, with surface temperatures around 50,000 degrees and more, shine with a bluish light.

91 How did the stars get their colors?

The color a star is to be during most of its life is determined by how much matter is packed into the star when it is formed. Stars are formed out of huge clouds of gas and dust. The gas is mostly hydrogen with a sprinkling of other elements, mainly helium. Stars 10 or more times as massive as the Sun become *blue giant* stars. They have core temperatures of 20 million degrees and higher, and surface temperatures of 50,000 degrees or more. Their high surface temperature makes them shine with a "hot" bluish white light. The star Rigel in the constellation Orion is one such star.

Medium-mass stars such as the Sun have core temperatures of about 15 million degrees and surface temperatures of about 6,000 degrees. Their medium surface temperature makes these stars shine with a "cooler" yellowish white light. Low-mass stars, such as the one called Ross 128, have core temperatures of only 10 million degrees and surface temperatures of only 3,000 degrees. Their low surface temperature makes these stars shine with an even "cooler" red light.

The medium- and high-mass stars all seem destined to pass through a stage when they swell up as giant stars that shine with red light, and are called red giants (see Questions 29 and 82).

92 How were the stars made?

Stars are formed out of super-large clouds of gas and dust. Most of the gas is hydrogen, along with a relatively small amount of helium. Stars formed out of these relatively "pure" clouds of hydrogen are called *Population II* stars.

Supernova and nova stars (see Question 88) cast matter off into space. When a supernova star explodes, the gases in its tremendously hot core form many elements heavier than hydrogen. Sometimes this ejected mixture of heavy elements is cast far across space and mixes with a relatively pure cloud of hydrogen. Stars that form out of these enriched clouds of matter are called *Population I* stars. The Sun is a Population I star formed out of secondhand matter some five billion years ago. So Earth and all its life forms contain matter that once helped a supernova star shine.

93 What's a black hole, and are there any in our galaxy?

When a supernova star explodes (see Question 88) all that is left of it is a huge ball of atomic particles called neutrons (see Question 26). Since neutrons are electrically neutral, they can be packed very closely together, because they do not repel one another. This means that such a neutron star is fantastically dense. Although a neutron star may contain as much matter as the Sun, it may be only a few miles in diameter. A lump of neutron star matter the size of a sugar cube would weight 10 million tons on Earth.

When the outer matter of a giant star collapses in on the core, the object contracts. Whatever rotation it had before is speeded up many times (see Question 58). Such a rapidly rotating neutron star is called a *pulsar* whenever it pulses, usually in radio waves. The bright object at the center of the Crab Nebula (see page 67) is the remains of a supernova explosion and one of the most rapidly rotating pulsars known. It rotates at the rate of about 30 times a second. There are other such rapidly rotating pulsars.

A pulsar's rapid rotation gradually slows. Eventually it slows enough for the star to collapse gravitationally once again. This collapse is a very rapid one, taking perhaps less than a second. The star is now even denser than before. A chunk the size of a sugar cube would now weigh a billion tons. The pull of gravity at the surface of one of these super-dense stars is so strong that no energy whatever can escape from the star—not even light. We will, therefore, never be able to see one of these fascinating objects, since it would simply be a black "hole" in space. And that is what astronomers call those massive blue giant stars that evolve into red giants, then explode as supernova stars, and finally collapse into oblivion: *black holes*.

Astronomers invented black holes, just as they invented black dwarfs (see Questions 29 and 90) and neutron stars. Although some astronomers deny that black holes exist, others say that black holes can be detected, even though we can't see them. Anything near a black hole gets pulled into it. A black hole with a companion star pulls gases away from the companion with such energy that X rays are given off. Detection of such X ray sources may indicate the presence of a black hole. It now seems that the X ray source Cygnus X1 may be a black hole, and there are other candidates in our galaxy. Some think that the center of our galaxy may be a black hole.

94 What's the Big Bang Theory?

According to the *Big Bang Theory,* between 12 and 20 billion years ago the entire Universe was an incredibly dense "primeval atom." This "atom" exploded with tremendous force, and all matter and space began expanding at speeds nearly that of light.

Between 100,000 and a million years after the Big Bang, enormous clouds of hydrogen and helium began to form. These were the only two elements in existence then. The clouds of gas became the galaxies. Eventually star formation began. It seems that all the galaxies formed during the first few billion years after the Big Bang.

The first stars to form in those early galaxies were high-mass stars that became supernova stars (see Question 88). On exploding, the supernova stars enriched surrounding nebulae with heavy elements (see Question 92). Later generations of stars, like the Sun, formed out of these enriched nebulae and so contain a wide variety of elements.

95 Where is the Universe going? Someone said it's expanding.

In every direction of the sky we look we see countless numbers of galaxies, some near, some far. By studying their light we can tell that all of the galaxies are rushing away from us, giving us the false impression that our galaxy is motionless at the center of the Universe. But our view of such an *expanding Universe* would be the same from any galaxy we happened to be in. We would still see all the other galaxies rushing away from us.

96 Is there an end to the Universe?

All of the galaxies we can see appear to be rushing away from us in a process of expansion. Astronomers wonder what the expanding Universe means. Did the expansion begin with the Big Bang (see Question 94)? And will the Universe just keep on expanding forever? Or will something stop it? If the Universe is dense enough, or has enough matter, gravitational attraction will slow down the expansion and reverse it, just as Earth's gravity slows down and reverses a handful of marbles tossed high into the air. Like the marbles, eventually the galaxies would slow down, stop and hang motionless for an instant, and then begin falling inward.

If gravitational braking and a reversal of the expansion does take place, all the galaxies will tumble together again in a "Big Squeeze" billions of years from now. The Big Squeeze may form another cosmic egg that will explode in another Big Bang and start the process all over again. This is the *oscillating Universe* theory. Some astronomers call it the Bang-Bang-Bang Theory.

One trouble with this idea of a Universe forming and destroying itself in cycles is that the Universe may not be dense enough to stop the present expansion. Perhaps we live in a Universe that will expand away forever and simply run down, never to be reborn.

⑨⑦ What are variable stars?

There are many types of *variable stars,* most of which are in advanced stages of their lives. All have cycles of brightening, dimming, and then brightening again. About 18,000 or so variables have been spotted in our galaxy, and telescopes reveal many variables in other galaxies. In fact, astronomers use some of those variables as a means of measuring the distance to other galaxies. Supernovae and nova stars (see Question 88) and shell stars (see Question 98) belong to a group called *explosive variables*. There also are *pulsating variables*. Those are the ones that go through regular cycles of brightening and dimming.

Most of the pulsating variables we know about are of the *Mira* type, named after the first such star discovered, Mira, in the constellation Cetus. Their typical *period,* or time of completing one cycle of going from dim to bright and back to dim again, is 300 days. During a period, a Mira-type variable star becomes about 15 times brighter than when it is dimmest.

RR Lyrae variables have periods of from 6 to 18 hours. Astronomers have seen more than 3,000 in our home galaxy. The best-known pulsating variables are the *Cepheid* type, named after the first such star observed, in the constellation Cepheus. These are among the largest stars in our galaxy and have periods ranging from a few days to about 50 days. Variable stars are not well understood. Amateur astronomers have made many important contributions to our knowledge of variable stars by identifying several of them and by measuring their periods. Usually, the big observatory telescopes are busy doing work considered more important than keeping track of variable stars.

98 What are shell stars?

Certain stars rotate so rapidly that they eject matter off into space. The matter then forms a shell around the star, so the star is called a *shell star*. The one shown in the photograph here is in the constellation Aquarius. It appears to be a ring around the central star. Actually it is a shell; it appears as a ring because we are looking through a greater thickness of matter out around the edge of the shell than when we look through the shell to its center. This particular shell of gas is expanding at the rate of about 10 miles a second. What makes shell stars explosively eject matter off into space is not well understood.

The shell of lighted gas around the central star actually is balloon shaped and encloses the central star. This is an example of a so-called planetary nebula, visible in the constellation Aquarius. (Hale Observatories)

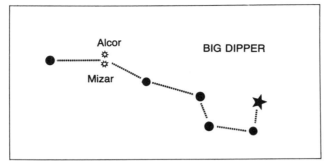

The middle star in the handle of the Big Dipper, Mizar, is an optical double star. Although it appears to be closely associated with Alcor, it is not. Their apparent closeness is due to a line-of-sight effect.

99 What's a double star?

About half the stars we can see are *double stars,* two stars held in gravitational association with each other and revolving around a common center. They also are called *binary stars*. The middle star of the three making up the Big Dipper's handle, Mizar, is a double star. If you look at Mizar just the right way you will see a faint star, Alcor, that appears to be associated with it, but is not. Some star systems, such as the one to which Alpha Centauri belongs, have three or more stars held in association by gravitation and are known as multiple-star systems. One rather interesting one can be found in the constellation Lyra. The star just to the left of the star Vega is called Epsilon Lyrae. To the unaided eye it appears as a single star, but binoculars reveal it as a double star. If you look at it through a small telescope you will see that each star forming the binocular pair is itself a double.

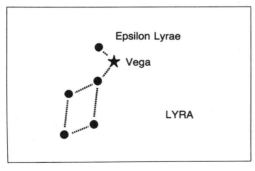

Epsilon Lyrae is located in the constellation Lyra the harp, as shown at left. The naked eye sees it as a single star, while binoculars reveal it as a double star, and a telescope shows it to be twin doubles.

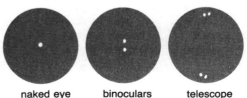

naked eye   binoculars   telescope

100 *Why does Earth have seasons?*

Because Earth's axis is tilted with respect to the plane of its orbit, parts of the planet at certain times receive the Sun's rays more directly than other parts. When the north pole of the axis is tilted away from the Sun, the Northern Hemisphere receives the Sun's rays at an angle; we call this period winter. When the north pole is tilted toward the Sun, the Northern Hemisphere receives the Sun's rays in a direct line; we call this period summer. Many people think that summer and winter are caused by the *distance* of Earth from the Sun. This is not so. Actually, in winter (January) in the Northern Hemisphere, Earth is closer to the Sun than it is in summer (June).

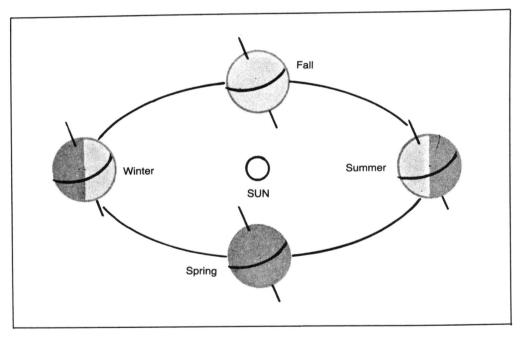

The tilt of Earth's axis of 23.5 degrees causes the seasons. When the Northern Hemisphere is tilted down and receives the direct rays of the Sun, we have summer. Six months later, the Northern Hemisphere is tilted up and receives the Sun's rays less directly, bringing on winter.

101 What's infinity, and how big is it?

Infinity can be defined as a larger number than anyone can think of. Some astronomers think that the Universe is infinite in size, meaning that it has no end. Galaxies go on and on forever into the endless distance. And the Universe is without beginning and without end. It has always existed and will exist forever. The mind cannot cope with such thoughts, which are utterly beyond our experience and beyond the ability of our imaginations to resolve.

If you tell me that the Universe is *finite,* or has a boundary, then I will ask you what is on the other side of the boundary. If you answer, ''nothing,'' then I will ask you what ''nothing'' is. If you say it is ''empty space,'' then I will have you trapped and will ask to what distance that empty space extends and if it is capable of containing matter—and there goes your boundary. So you see there is no end to the Universe; at least we cannot think of one.

Index